M000313385

Cyberpunk City
Book Three
The Blayze War

D.L. Young

Cover art by Ignacio Bazan-Lazcano

For free books, new release updates, exclusive previews and content, visit dlyoungfiction.com

If you're losing your soul and you know it, then
you've still got a soul to lose.

— Charles Bukowski

1
WINNER TAKE NOTHING

"Mr. Wonderful's here." Zanne the waitress leaned in close as she removed an empty glass from the table.

Maddox sighed at the news. And it had been such a nice evening too. He scanned the bar's main room. "Where?"

"He's still up front," she said. "Asking if you're here."

"He alone?" Maddox asked.

The waitress cocked an eyebrow. "Is he ever?"

She leaned in closer, her yellow dreadlocks nearly touching him. Fishnet thighs pressed against the tabletop. "You want me to get rid of him?"

Maddox shook his head. "Don't bother."

"You got it, boss. Do you need anything else?" she asked, still so close he felt her breath warm on his face. "Anything I can give you?" she added suggestively.

"I'm good, thanks."

Her flirtations had begun months ago, when Maddox had bought the place. He'd never reciprocated, but it didn't seem to bother her or lessen her own advances.

Drink tray in her hand, she sauntered away as Tommy arrived. The kid slid into the booth and gawked at the waitress's swaying hips.

"I don't know why you don't hit that, bruh. I would so hit that if I were you. I would so, so hit that."

Maddox lit a cigarette, blew smoke. "I'm trying to run a professional joint here, kid. That kind of thing's bad for business."

"Bad for business," Tommy echoed, nodding sagely. "Yeah, that makes sense."

Maddox surveyed the bar from his corner booth. Foot-high holos projected from inlaid devices on each table. Talking heads of newsreaders. Brazilian soccer matches. Gangbangs from live sex feeds.

The walls were set to a beach scene from Bali. A vast turquoise seascape. Towering palm trees, fronds fluttering in the breeze. Other nights featured a vast Andean plain, rust brown and rocky with distant snowcapped peaks. Or a street scene from another city. Jakarta or Kobe or Moscow.

Winner Take Nothing had an early-evening crowd and a late crowd. The early arrivals were well dressed, wealthy, and snobbish. Company types, mostly. Well-compensated corporati who spent their days in highfloor executive suites and board rooms. The one-percenters, just as demanding and self-important as he remembered them from his brief tenure in the corporate world. They bitched about prices and grabbed the waitresses' asses when they got drunk. But they spent money like water and never broke out into fistfights. So all things considered, they were a pretty easy crowd to handle, once you got past their pretensions.

The late crowd came from a different segment of City society, one just as affluent but organized along different lines than the matrixed structure of a global corporation. This crowd had no vice presidents, no board members, no highfloor government officials. They were the City's criminal class, its elite underworld of prosperous embezzlers, narcos, pimps, smugglers, and data thieves. They mixed well with the patrons from the legitimate world. In fact, for some it was difficult to distinguish the criminals from the noncriminals. Not for Maddox, though. His underworld brethren might dress like highfloor corporati; they might speak like them, even act like them. But the lawless among his patrons always had a slightly different air about them. A kind of vibe only the streetwise emitted, like some pheromone others of their kind recognized with ease. A wariness, or maybe awareness was the right word. A perpetual awareness, a sharp sense of their surroundings. The keen, never-resting perception of a predator, constantly searching out prey, sizing up the herd to find its weakest members.

At half past ten o'clock, the bar's patrons seemed evenly distributed between the two crowds. The early arrivals had ebbed, their numbers replaced with a flow of latecomers. The white-collar types who stayed later got a thrill out of mixing with the City's upper-crust gangsters. It was part of the bar's appeal, Maddox had come to understand. Want to rub elbows with the City's criminal elite? Hit Winner Take Nothing around midnight.

The bar was the first aboveboard business Maddox had owned in his life—a legal milestone in his otherwise illegitimate career as a datajacker. After a short stint at a biotech firm—the only legit job he'd ever held prior to being a bar owner—he'd gone back to datajacking, the illegal trade he'd been immersed in since his teens. With sweat and grit and a bit of good luck, he'd managed to find his sweet spot in the black market. The jobs had begun to roll in, and so had the money. With the cash piling up, investing in a legit business had seemed like a good call. At thirty-two, he was old for a datajacker. Those in his profession rarely made it to thirty before getting caught or killed. At some point he knew he'd have to quit the game and find some other livelihood. So when the bar's previous owner—an old contact fleeing the country to dodge a bribery charge—had offered to sell Maddox the place for pennies on the dollar, the datajacker had jumped at the chance.

A throng of new customers poured through the main room's entryway, and the low murmur of conversation grew into a restless din of raised voices. Dezmund Parcells—or Mr. Wonderful as the staff had sarcastically dubbed him—marched into the bar with all the discretion of a street parade. Overdressed as always in a three-piece suit complete with gold-chained timepiece tucked into a pocket, Dezmund was trailed by his entourage, a dozen or so of his crew and hangers-on. Employees and sycophants who followed him everywhere, laughing at his every joke and buzzing about him like moths around a streetlamp. Or flies around shit, Maddox reflected.

"Oh, great," Tommy sighed, mirroring Maddox's earlier reaction. "Mr. Wonderful's here."

For all the hands he shook as he made his way to the bar, you would have thought Dezmund was running for office. For a moment Maddox considered slipping out of a side exit, but then stubbornly decided against it. This was his place, after all.

As he worked the room, Dezmund glanced furtively in Maddox's direction a couple times but made no immediate move in his direction. That would be too obvious, too needy. Instead, he maneuvered his followers to the bar, where they ordered drinks and he pretended not to notice the tavern's owner for the next fifteen minutes. Finally, Dezmund made eye contact, feigned surprise, and lifted his drink in the datajacker's direction. Maddox returned the gesture with a nod.

"Oh, man," Tommy complained as he noticed Dezmund moving in their direction. "I can't stand this fook. Look at him. Look how he's dressed. Like he's some big shot corporati or something. He's just a jacker like you and me, this guy."

"Take it easy," Maddox said, blowing smoke. "Giving him free rent in your head doesn't help anything."

"That another Rooneyism?" this kid asked.

"Saw it on a self-help feed," Maddox joked.

The kid looked confused for a moment, then chuckled. Six months back—after they'd managed to dodge a frame-up for a terrorist bombing—Maddox had taken on Tommy as his apprentice, the same way Rooney had taken him on way back when. The kid was a quick study and had the innate talent every datajacker needed to handle the demands of virtual space. But he could be a handful at times. If he wasn't bouncing off the walls with adolescent mania, he was picking Maddox's brain for hours on end about countermeasures and sledgehammer executables and razorwall applications. Tommy Park, datajacker-in-training, was a bundle of manic energy wrapped in street kid bluster. Maddox sometimes wondered if Rooney had thought the same about him once upon a time.

Dezmund's retinue followed in his wake as he made his way over, a woman on each arm. Arriving at the table, he removed his specs, handed them to the blonde on his left, and smiled graciously down at Maddox.

"Blackburn," he said, reaching out a hand. "Good to see you, old friend."

Maddox half-stood as he shook the proffered hand. "Dez," he said. "You remember Tommy." Maddox tilted his head toward the kid.

Dezmund gave Tommy the smallest of nods before fixing his gaze again on Maddox. "How's the bar business treating you?"

Maddox blew smoke. "Can't complain. How's business for you?"

"Couldn't be better," Dezmund said. "Then again," he added, "I guess it could be a bit better if you'd stop undercutting me."

Maddox held Dezmund's gaze, tried not to react. "Undercutting you? Not sure I know what you're talking about."

Dezmund grinned. "You used to be a better liar, Blackburn."

"I'll have to work on that," Maddox said.

"You're stealing from me," Dezmund said, the smile vanishing. "Don't sit there and deny it."

"Hey, bruh!" Tommy exclaimed, springing up from his seat. A street instinct from a street kid. Winner Take Nothing was his mentor's home turf, and you didn't disrespect someone on their home turf and get away with it. Maddox grasped the kid's arm, then shook his head at him. Tommy reluctantly took his seat again, glaring at Dezmund like a guard dog ready to pounce on an intruder.

"Last time I checked," Maddox said, "the black market was a market just like any other, and vendors can bid whatever they want."

"Don't give me that bullshit," Dezmund said. "There's a difference between bidding low and stealing business, and you know it."

Maddox did know it. There *was* a difference. A big difference.

When a potential datajacking gig hit the radar—through either the underground feeds or word of mouth or a paid go-between—the hiring party sometimes sought bids from different crews. Some did this because they were cheap or cash-strapped. These clients invariably went with the lowest bidder. Others simply wanted a price comparison to make sure their first quote wasn't a rip-off. The bids themselves usually fell into a predictable range. Newbie crews with low cred and not much rep bid low, and the more experienced shops charged a premium for their proven expertise. There were no rules to the bidding process. The black market was a brutally efficient free-for-all, and you played the game at your own risk.

There were, however, standards most datajackers followed, unwritten codes of behavior respected by all. You never sold out another jacker to the cops, for example. If a rival screwed you over, you took care of it yourself. You had their legs broken or you recruited away their best talent or—in extreme cases—you had them knocked off. But you never went to the cops, ever. Another no-no was stealing business with an undercutting bid at the last minute. In competitive situations, you bid what you could afford to, period. You didn't come in late and quote half the market rate. And if you did that sort of thing often enough, you shouldn't plan on staying around very long. Disruptive lowballers were swiftly run out of the business by larger established shops with threats of violence or, if that didn't work, actual violence.

"Let's talk in my office," Maddox suggested.

"What's wrong with right here?" Dezmund countered.

"What's your damage, bruh?" Tommy snarled. "Show the house some respect or get out of here."

Dezmund tightened his lips and shook his head disapprovingly. "If this is how you treat all your guests, Blackburn, I'm afraid this place isn't going to stay in business very long." Then to Tommy: "You should be careful how you talk to people, kid."

The kid sprung up from his chair. "You can't give me orders. You're not my boss. Why don't you take your sad-ass crew and get out of—"

"Tommy," Maddox snapped. "Bring it down a few notches. We're just having a parley here, yeah?"

By now, much of the conversation in the bar had stopped. Customers and employees peered over at Maddox's booth with tense, expectant stares.

"Sad-ass crew?" Dezmund said. He half-turned to his entourage. "You hear that? The boy here thinks I've got a sad-ass crew." His gang laughed derisively in response. "And what would you call your crew?" Dezmund asked the kid. "Your two-man crew that has to steal like some starving kid robbing apples from a fruit stand?"

"We're ten times the jackers any of you are," the kid shot back.

"You really think so?" Dezmund asked.

"Hells, yeah," Tommy said defiantly. The kid was in a full-blown froth now.

Dezmund lifted an eyebrow at Maddox. "Care to prove it, then?" He smiled in a way that managed to be at once playful and threatening.

"Prove it how?" Maddox asked.

"You know how," Dezmund said. "The way we used to way back when."

"You're joking, right?"

"Why not?" Again the ambiguous smile. "Unless you're scared."

Now it was Maddox's turn to grin. "Let's do it."

2
DEZMUND

The suit-and-tied patrons of Winner Take Nothing hadn't expected to see a real live datajacking contest that night, so when the staff pulled together a couple tables and began to break out decks and trodebands and holo projectors, a wave of excitement ran through the bar. Even the criminal types among the evening's customers, the thieves and fences and hustlers and black marketeers, became wrapped up in the buzzing anticipation. Most had only seen this kind of thing in movies on the entertainment feeds: an old-school datajacker showdown.

When the staff finished setting up the gear a minute later, the bar's atmosphere had completely changed. Normally quiet and low-key, Winner Take Nothing had transformed into a noisy, raucous scene, reminding Maddox of the excitable vibe of underground fighting matches.

Dezmund looked over the setup with a critical eye and a knitted brow. "Not exactly top-of-the-line gear, is it? But I suppose we can work with it."

"All right, then." Maddox gripped Tommy around

the shoulder. "The kid's ready. Winner buys drinks for the house, yeah?" He made sure this last was loud enough for the entire bar to hear. A chorus of yeahs and all rights and applause filled the air. He glanced at the kid, found Tommy's eyes wide in shock.

"Me?" the kid gasped. "I thought *you* were going to—"

"It's his best versus my best. That's how these things always go down. You knew that, right?"

"Yeah, sure," Tommy said hesitantly. "Of course I knew that." The poor kid looked like he was about to be thrown into a pit of starving lions. Which wasn't far from the truth, now that Maddox thought about it. In large operations like Dez's, head-to-head jacker contests were part of the workaday routine. Challenges were thrown down every day, serving as a kind of brutal in-house Darwinism. Those with the best records secured bragging rights and the top spot in a crew's pecking order. Dez's top dog would have hundreds of hours of experience in these types of contests. Tommy Park, on the other hand, was a different story. As the only understudy in a two-person shop, the kid's experience was limited to automated scenarios. The kid had done pretty well in those environments, but Maddox knew taking on another living, breathing person was different. Especially in front of a crowd.

The bar's patrons applauded and cheered. They were ready for a show. Maddox leaned close to the kid's ear. "You can do it, kid. Trust me."

Whether it was the crowd's urging or his own words that lifted the kid's spirits, Maddox couldn't say, but in the next moment a cocky smile came across Tommy's face. He rubbed his palms together.

"Let's goooo," he said, strutting forward, chest out and smiling. Louder applause and cheering broke out as he swung his leg over the chair and sat down.

The kid's opponent emerged from the back of Dezmund's retinue. Short and unassuming, she had a bob of sandy-brown hair colored blood red at the tips. Her name was Blayze, an up-and-comer Maddox had heard mentioned more and more lately in datajacking circles. He'd never met her, but word had it she was Dezmund's top talent. She looked nineteen, twenty at most, making her Tommy's senior by some five years. Behind a pair of Venturelli specs, her face was relaxed and composed, a tiny island of calm in the excited storm of the bar's buzzing patrons. She locked eyes with her benefactor, lifting her brows in an unspoken question. Dezmund responded with a small nod: permission granted. The girl then stepped forward to a frenzy of hoots and howls, wearing an oversized leather jacket with a large smiley face covering most of the back. She removed her specs, turned the chair around backwards, then sat down and picked up one of the two trodebands. If she was rattled by the rowdy scene around her, her steely expression betrayed no sign of it.

Dezmund leaned close to Maddox. "Your boy's in big trouble."

"It wouldn't be the first time."

Maddox watched as Tommy egged the crowd on, cupping his hand behind his ear and squinting like he could hardly hear them, like their cheers weren't nearly loud enough for someone of his awesome talent. The bar's customers responded, their chants growing louder as they clapped and whistled and stomped their feet. Tommy Park had the spotlight, and he was loving every moment of it. Maddox couldn't help but smile at the kid's bravado. It was an utterly misguided confidence, of course, but that didn't diminish its entertainment value. The kid was a born ham.

The contest rules were simple: two datajackers plugged into an offline digital environment, a simulated datasphere or some other purpose-built domain designed to test their skills. Once the clock started, whoever completed the designated task first was the winner. Most often, the objective was to find a simulated datasphere's vulnerability, exploit it, and steal some predetermined dataset. All without getting detected, of course. A short-range wireless broadcast allowed spectators to watch each avatar's perspective on their specs.

As the two datajackers readied themselves, adjusting their trodebands and firing up their decks, the crowd of onlookers donned their specs and toggled over to the broadcast feed. Maddox and Dezmund scrolled through a menu of DS simulations on a small holo monitor projected above the table, finally agreeing on a recent submission to the library by a game designer known for his tough, realistic creations.

The simulation was loaded into the shared environment, and a timer counted down on every pair of specs in the bar. When it reached five seconds, the crowd shouted out the numbers, each one louder than the last.

"THREE...TWO...ONE...GO!!!"

In less than a minute it was over. And it went pretty much as Maddox had expected.

The ham got schooled.

*   *   *

"I told you she was good," Dezmund said, still basking in the glow of his victory. He sipped his free shot of whiskey, savoring it a moment before swallowing.

"You didn't lie," Maddox said.

They sat alone in Maddox's small office in the back of the bar. Through the closed door came muffled tones of conversation and the low, thudding beat of technopop.

"So how's business?" Dezmund asked.

"Not bad. Not getting rich running a saloon, mind you, but I can't complain."

"I wasn't talking about your side hustle," Dezmund clarified.

"Ah," Maddox said, lighting a cigarette. "Same thing. No complaints."

"How many do you have on the payroll these days? It's not really just you and the kid, is it?"

Maddox blew smoke. "It is, actually. Just the two of us."

Dezmund shook his head as if he was disappointed to hear it. "Blackburn, Blackburn. You gotta think about the future. Our business is no different from any other. If you're not growing, you're dying."

"More crew means more headaches." Maddox shrugged. "And who needs that?"

Dezmund nodded in agreement. "Won't disagree with you there. You'd be amazed how much time I spend breaking up melodramas." He lifted the glass, finished off the whiskey. "Price of success, I suppose."

Maddox took a long drag, resisted the urge to roll

his eyes at the humble-bragging. Yes, yes, you're the big shot in the room, he was tempted to say. You have a bigger crew, you live on a higher floor, blah blah blah. Could this guy's dick be any smaller?

"Still," Dezmund went on, "maybe if you had a bigger crew you could quote more bids and not have to steal business from me."

Maddox blew smoke. He didn't bother to deny what they both knew was true. He had indeed won business by undercutting Dezmund, and he'd done it on more than one occasion. After he'd bought Winner Take Nothing and reopened its doors to the public, those first several months had been shaky ones, financially speaking. Running a bar was expensive, as Maddox had learned, and the place wasn't coming close to breaking even. Desperate for cash, Maddox lowballed a few deals, snatching them from Dezmund's grasp. More than a few deals, if he was being honest.

So, yes, the man sitting in front of him had every right to be righteously angry at his competitor, but at the moment, for whatever reason, he didn't appear to be.

"Just want you know I'm not here to give you hell about all that," Dezmund said, then added, "though I probably should."

"You seemed pretty pissed about it earlier," Maddox pointed out.

Dezmund shrugged. "Just playing to the crowd. Can't let my crew think I've gone soft, can I?"

"God forbid."

"I'm here about an opportunity, something we can both profit from. A once-in-a-lifetime job. I'm talking really good money, Blackburn."

"Interesting," Maddox said, though he wasn't moved. Every datajacker he'd ever known occasionally—and some more often than others—fell victim to a kind of criminal overoptimism. A misguided conviction that their next job would be the best one ever, the Big One, the impossibly lucrative windfall they'd been waiting for their entire crooked life. Even Maddox, sober and skeptical by nature, had fallen into the same trap once or twice, overestimating some gig's upside while looking past the downside.

"Why do you need my help?" Maddox asked. He lifted his chin toward the door. "Looks like you have plenty in-house talent."

"I do," Dezmund agreed. "They're very good. But this gig needs...specific experience."

"Meaning?"

"It's a brokerage house."

Maddox took a long, contemplative draw. "Which one?"

"BNO Commerz."

Maddox blew smoke and fought back the urge to laugh. There was overly ambitious, and then there was just plain stupid. For Maddox, the idea of robbing a company like BNO fit squarely into the latter category.

BNO Commerz was the largest financial brokerage firm in the world. And like every large global company involved in banking or investment trading, they spent billions on data security. Banks and brokerage firms and other financial institutions were in the trust business, and if customers were going to let them manage huge sums of their money, they needed to be one hundred percent sure there was zero possibility of some data thief sneaking in and emptying their accounts.

"You're joking," Maddox said.

"I'm not."

"Come on," Maddox scoffed. "BNO's a top-five bank. You know how tight they lock down their DSes. They spend a fortune to keep our dirty little hands out of their cookie jar. Those places have the biggest, meanest AIs around." Financial firms' dataspheres were the most secure, most impenetrable virtual environments that existed. Maddox had never heard of anyone breaching the DS of a top financial company like BNO. The very idea was lunacy. Like thinking you could break through a bank's vault door with a carpenter's hammer.

Dezmund sat there silently, a hint of a smile on his face. Then it hit Maddox.

"You've got an in," he said.

"I've got an in," Dezmund repeated.

That might make things different, Maddox reflected. *Might.*

"I'm listening," he said, tapping his cigarette over the ashtray.

Dezmund leaned forward. "I've had a plant in their data security department for a year."

"A plant?" Maddox said in disbelief. "How'd you get someone from your crew past an employment screen?"

"That's the beauty of it," Dezmund said. "We didn't have to clean her history at all. She came to us, right out of college. Zero criminal background. She just didn't want to work in the legit world. Wanted to run with a datajacking crew." He chuckled. "Kids today. Go figure."

"Sounds too good to be true."

"Exactly what I thought, until we checked her out. She was clean and pristine. Top grades, even. So I think to myself, what's the best way to use someone with a spotless record, right out of school with a degree in cybersecurity?"

"Plant her in a big firm," Maddox said, finishing the thought.

"Exactly. And she's spent the past year getting herself into a spot where she can help me." He leaned in closer. "Now, BNO announces its earning results in four days. And anyone who knows those results before they're public stands to clean up in the markets."

Maddox smoked thoughtfully as he listened. Stealing earnings results before they went public wasn't a new scam. Dealing in inside information had probably been around as long as publicly traded markets had. And while Maddox rarely invested in stocks and bonds—like most criminals, he preferred the liquidity of hard cash and cash-based accounts—he knew enough about the markets to be skeptical. He reminded Dezmund how government agencies had AIs watching for unusual buying and selling activity before earnings calls, and how highfloor traders and executives—people with far more market sophistication than datajackers—got busted all the time for insider trading.

"That's the beauty of it," Dezmund said. "I'm not going to buy or sell a single share. I've got a hedge fund manager on the line. I come through with the goods, he'll pay." He went on, explaining how he'd invested months setting the whole thing up. He'd profiled dozens of hedge fund managers, narrowing them down to a single potential customer: a Swiss national with the perfect mix of moral flexibility and an impeccable reputation.

Dezmund had carefully approached the fund manager, and once the man had been convinced the datajacker wasn't some scam artist, he'd seized the opportunity to earn an easy billion or two.

"I got the feeling," Dezmund said, "it wasn't the first time he'd dealt in inside info."

"Does he know who you are?" Maddox asked.

Dezmund gave him a disdainful look. "Please, Blackburn. You think I'd show my face on something this big?"

"People take risks when there's a lot of money involved."

"Well, I'm not one of them, and you ought to know that. Crooks like us don't make it this long in this business if we show our faces to the clients, do we? It was all set up with blind go-betweens and quantum-encrypted calls, same as always."

Maddox didn't sense Dezmund was lying. He reminded himself the man sitting across from him might be a strutting peacock who shamelessly basked in his infamy, but when it came down to business, he wasn't the kind to cut corners or take unnecessary risks. Dez was a top pro. Vain and show-offy as fuck, but still a top pro.

He gazed at Maddox for a long moment, as if he was trying to gauge his colleague's interest. "So are you in?"

A ribbon of bluish smoke rose from the tip of Maddox's cigarette. He couldn't deny he was intrigued. The man had done his homework, and it was clearly going to be a lucrative job.

Still, banks were risky. Life-and-death kind of

risky. Even if you had someone holding the door open for you or distracting the company's guard dog AI while you snuck in, there were still lots of other nasty defensive apps and countermeasures waiting to jump on you.

And then there was the obvious question, which Maddox went ahead and voiced.

"You've been setting this up for a year," he said. "Why bring me in at the eleventh hour?"

A sheepish look came over Dezmund's features. It was a rare crack in the man's unwavering confidence.

"This is the biggest job I've ever taken on," he admitted. "And I'd be lying if I told you I wasn't worried about it. You're the only one I know who's ever breached a bank or taken on an AI. And even though I've got my insider, it's still a bank, and I'd feel a lot better about things if I had you on the crew for this one."

Maddox turned it over. The bar wasn't an anchor around his neck anymore. The place was making money these days, though only by the thinnest of margins. He wasn't the desperate cash-strapped Maddox he'd been a few months ago. Still, the opportunist in him hated to let a big payday slip away.

"I don't know if I can take some teenager telling me what to do," he said.

"You don't have to worry about that," Dezmund said. "I'll keep them in line."

Maddox blew smoke. "I'll have to think about it."

Dezmund's features dropped in disappointment. "You'll have to think about it." He nodded slowly. "You do that, Blackburn. You think about it. And I'll think about whether or not I care about those jobs you stole from me."

Maddox winced inwardly. He had known at some point Dezmund would play that card, and he had no counter for it.

There were unwritten rules among datajackers. Things you did and didn't do. Undercutting a competitor once or twice, for example, was no big deal. Everybody did that kind of thing once in a while. But if you did it too often, and to the wrong party, you could end up in a trash dumpster with a bullet in your head. Maddox had assumed Dezmund's operation was so large, so lucrative, that the man wouldn't care about a few lost deals. But apparently he'd hitched a ride on Dezmund's coattails one too many times, and now he was expected to make amends, to repay the debt.

Maddox cursed himself for being lazy, for stealing deals instead of putting in the time and effort to drum up his own business. For giving Dezmund leverage over him. He could almost see Rooney shaking his head at him, telling him he'd made his bed, and now he had to sleep in it.

Mashing out his cigarette, he sighed. He owed the man sitting across from him. Whether he liked it or not.

"All right," he said. "I'm in."

3
HELLO, SALARYMAN

Well past midnight, Winner Take Nothing's throbbing technopop had been silenced, and the place had cleared out except for one last customer, drunk and passed out in a corner booth. The suited corporati, who'd apparently had two or three too many, snored deeply. The man's mouth gaped open and his cheek was pressed against the tabletop.

Sitting on a barstool, Maddox pondered what exactly he'd signed up for, debating whether or not he should try to get out of it. Dezmund had assured him there would be a nice payout, and for his efforts Maddox would receive a generous portion. He'd also made sure Maddox understood that helping with this job would balance the ledger between them. That whatever bad blood Maddox's deal-stealing had caused, all would be forgiven. Still, with all the upsides, Maddox couldn't help dwelling on the downsides. The risk to life and limb, the risk of getting busted. And beyond all that, there was something else, some intangible thing poking at his gut. Something about this job that felt wrong.

The unconscious corporati's snoring finally grew loud enough to interrupt Maddox's second-guessing. The datajacker lit a cigarette and gestured to Feng, the massive bouncer who was halfway through his closing duties, wiping down tables with a rag and a bottle of spray cleaner.

"Got it, boss," Feng said, setting down the bottle and tossing the rag over his shoulder. Maddox subvocalized a command in his specs, calling a cab to take the man home. Feng lifted the drunken man gingerly and half-walked, half-carried the suit to the front door. Someone from outside opened the door and held it for them, entering the bar after the pair exited.

"We're closed," Maddox said to the silhouette standing in the entryway. Whoever it was didn't move.

The datajacker swiveled away from the bar and slid off the stool. "I said we're closed," he called, a bit louder.

As the woman stepped forward out of the shadow, a smile touched Maddox's lips. Apparently, this was his night for surprise visitors.

"Hello, salaryman," Beatrice said.

* * *

The next morning, in her rented suite on the sixty-second floor of the Royal Belmond, Beatrice lay next to him, propped up on an elbow, the sheets bunched around her waist. Below his own waist Maddox was sore. She'd worn him out in the best possible way: three exhausting rounds last night and another, gentler one this morning.

Her hair was different now, short-cropped and dyed blue, but the rest of her was the same as he remembered. Pale skin and lean, muscled limbs. Bright brown eyes that missed nothing. The small telltale iris flicker that gave them away as artificial implants. The softness of her breasts pressed against his side.

She was still based in Canada, she'd told him, and she was in town on a job. A freelance security gig for some trade official negotiating import tariffs with his American counterparts. Two nights, maybe three, depending on how the talks played out.

"It's not a law, you know," she said. "You don't have to do it." Last night she'd sensed he was preoccupied about something, and he'd told her about his first surprise visitor of the evening, and about what he'd agreed to.

"It's a street thing," he said, but from her eye-roll reaction he could see that wasn't nearly enough of an explanation. He gave her the wider context, recounting how he'd undercut Dezmund, stealing jobs out from under him at the last minute.

"So what's the big deal?" she said. "Isn't that how a free market's supposed to work?"

"Free market, right," Maddox said. "No market I've ever seen is free. And in the black market where I make a living, when you undercut another jacker, it makes for bad blood. And when there's enough bad blood, people get hurt."

"So why'd you steal from him in the first place?" she asked.

Why indeed. He reached over to the nightstand for a cigarette.

"Ah, ah, ah. Nonsmoking suite," Beatrice scolded, stopping him. Then she returned to her question. "So tell me."

"I needed quick cash," he explained. "When I bought the bar, the doors had been shut for a while. It took some time for people to find it again after we opened back up. It's doing fine now, but between buying it and keeping it afloat for a few months, things were tight for a while. Dezmund has the biggest operation around. At any given moment they're working three or four jobs at the same time, so I guess I figured—"

"He wouldn't miss the business."

"Yeah."

She shook her head at his carelessness, and he didn't blame her. It was a bad call, and deep down he'd probably known as much at the time. But sometimes the prospect of easy money clouded your thoughts, made you do things you ordinarily wouldn't. This was especially true when you had negative cash flow.

"So if you do this, you and he are square," she said.

"Right."

"And you can't just pay him back? Compensate him for the business you took?"

If only things were that simple, Maddox thought. "He's hot for this job, wants it really bad. And he needs all the help he can get." He sighed. "No, I painted myself into this corner. Playing ball's the only way out."

She stared at him for a long moment, wheels turning behind her eyes. "Have you considered the possibility this whole thing's a setup? Send you on some impossible job to get you busted, or worse. A ruse to get you out of the way for good."

It had indeed occurred to him, but the idea had

only been a fleeting one. "I don't see it."

"No?"

"His best talent's going to be plugging in with me. If it's a set up, he'd be putting them at risk too."

"What if they all jump you once you're inside?"

Maddox shrugged. "But why bother? If he really wanted to take me out, it's a lot easier to send a couple thugs to my bar. It's not like I'm hard to find these days."

"Maybe he's counting on you thinking exactly that so you don't see it coming. Maybe he's trying to gain your trust."

"He wouldn't bother trying to do that."

Beatrice smile wistfully. "Of course not," she said. "He knows you, doesn't he?"

The air in the suite chilled with the comment, which had nothing to do with Dezmund or the BNO job. The last time Maddox and Beatrice had been together, she'd invited him to leave the City with her and make a fresh start in Canada. For someone as guarded and private as Beatrice, it had been a rare moment of vulnerability. Maddox couldn't remember exactly how he'd worded his refusal, but he hadn't forgotten the uneasy moments that followed. It was as if a wall had immediately gone up between them. A wall he realized was still standing.

A timely knock on the door interrupted the awkward moment. Maddox hurriedly threw on his pants and opened the door to Tommy.

With gear bags slung over his shoulders, the kid stepped into the entryway, craning his neck around as he marveled at the luxury suite. "Nice digs, bruh," he said, whistling.

Beatrice appeared around a corner, tying the sash

on a short silk robe. The kid lowered the bags to the floor. "Hey, B. Long time no see. I dig the blue," he said, referring to her hair.

"Tommy Park," she said, smiling. "How's my favorite Anarchy Boy?"

"Aw, you know," the kid said. "Doing biz with the man."

"Not letting him get you into trouble, I hope," she said.

The kid's face dropped, and he shot Maddox an icy stare. "No," he said. "No trouble. Just throws me to the wolves sometimes and watches 'em eat me alive."

"You still pouting about that?" Maddox said.

"I'm not pouting," Tommy protested. "It's righteous rage, bruh. You let me get roasted on home turf, in front of everyone. How uncool is that?"

"Christ, salaryman," Beatrice said, "what the hell did you do to the kid?"

"Hung me out to dry," the kid snapped, "that's what."

Maddox longed for a cigarette. He gave Beatrice a helpless look. "I'd heard about this hotshot on Dezmund's crew. I wanted to see how good she really was, so I let the kid take her on. Now I know."

"Thanks to me getting owned," Tommy added.

"I'll make it up to you, kid," Maddox said, "I promise."

"I bet you Old Man Rooney never did you like that," the kid said, "did he?"

Well, shit. The kid had him on that one. No, Rooney hadn't ever hung Maddox out to dry, even when he might have had a good reason to. The kid's comment stung more than the datajacker wanted to

27

admit.

"Well, I'm not Roon," he said icily. "Am I?"

The kid seemed to sense he'd stepped over a line. Maddox took a calming breath and changed the subject. "You get everything I asked for?"

"And then some," the kid said, handing Maddox one of the bags. "Brought backups, too." He patted the bag he was still holding. "You know, just in case."

"Good," Maddox said. He'd forgotten to tell Tommy to bring backup gear, but the kid had prudently done it anyway. He might still be a novice datajacker, but the kid was definitely learning his trade.

Hanging from his shirt collar, Maddox's lenses began to chime. He put them on, blinked away the alert, and slung the gear bag over his shoulder.

"Come on, kid," he told Tommy. "Our ride's here."

4
PISSING CONTEST

Morning rush hour in the City. The limo merged into the clogged, slowly moving transit lanes. Above and below, countless hovers snaked along in tight formations, their autonav sensors invisibly linked, synchronizing each vehicle's acceleration and deceleration to optimize traffic flow. Maddox watched the City drift by: megastructure after megastructure, each with its own multicolored skin of graffiti tags and street murals reaching up thirty, forty, even fifty stories high in places. Locals called them hiverises, these conjoined, interconnected conglomerations of ancient buildings. Like some giant reef of concrete and steel, they formed the backbone of the massive archipelago simply known as the City, the continuous urban sprawl spanning over two hundred miles and home to over a hundred million residents, encompassing the old standalone cities of New York City, Newark, Philadelphia, Baltimore, and Washington, D.C.

Normally gray and overcast, the sky this morning was an uncharacteristic bright and cloudless blue.

Holo ads tens of stories high flickered dimly against building facades, their projections less effective and nearly transparent under the glare of direct sunlight. Next to Maddox, Tommy sat with his face pressed against the window, his breath making a fog smudge on the glass.

"Now this is what I call traveling in style," Tommy said.

For his part, Maddox was less impressed by the ride's soft leather seats, darkened windows, and roomy interior. Dezmund had always been a show-off, never missing an opportunity to flaunt his success, especially to anyone he considered a rival, like Maddox. Even back when they were teenagers and he couldn't afford such extravagances, Dezmund had clothed himself in knockoff designer suits and fake leather shoes. And now that he could afford the real thing, the Armani-clad hustler businessman had become his personal brand. Yes, the limo was a comfortable ride, but it was also Dez's not-so-subtle way of reminding Maddox who was the top dog in their little pack.

After a long, plodding descent through the traffic stack, they arrived at the meet, a gray-bricked lowrise in East Flatbush, Brooklyn. As the hover settled onto the rooftop landing pad, Maddox turned to the kid. "These people aren't friends. Don't forget that. I've known Dezmund for a long time, but that doesn't mean I trust him."

The kid gave Maddox a look, and the look said he knew what they were walking into, that he knew how to handle himself on rival turf, and that he didn't need to be warned about something so damned obvious in the first place.

"Just saying," Maddox added as a small concession, inwardly admitting his worry stemmed more from the job itself than any doubts he had about the kid. Tommy Park was a lot of things, but clueless wasn't one of them. In fact, his datajacking apprentice was far brighter than Maddox had initially given him credit for, demonstrating as much over these last months on several occasions, both inside virtual space and out. Sure, he was impulsive and overconfident at times, and far more chatty than Maddox cared for. But for the most part the kid was all right. And if Maddox was being honest with himself, he couldn't deny Tommy had grown on him.

When the doors lifted, Blayze was there to greet them. As if Tommy needed another reminder they weren't on friendly turf. She smiled broadly at the kid, a grin that struck Maddox as every bit as flirtatious as it was gloating. He'd have to keep an eye on this one, he told himself. She looked like trouble.

* * *

The workspace they'd use for the job consisted of several interconnected suites rented on the building's top floor. As they went down the rooftop stairwell, the address's shabby first impression—a beat-up exterior, pockmarked and covered in faded street art—was soon forgotten as the trio entered to find an elegant, well-appointed interior.

"They gutted the whole thing and refurbished last year," Blayze explained as she led them down the marble-tiled hallway. "A couple investors ran out of money before they started work on the outside, from what I hear."

They reached the end of the corridor and passed through a doorway. Inside the spacious suite, Maddox found the most expensive collection of gear he'd ever seen assembled in one place. He counted twenty VS decks, at least twice that many holo projectors, and half a dozen small cone-shaped chatter bubble casters. Stacks of trodebands still in their shrinkwrap lay atop a long dining table, as did an assortment of portable storage devices and small tool sets. Around ten youths, presumably Dezmund's top jackers, all in their late teens or early twenties, looked up from their work as the trio entered. After a long moment of icy stares, they slowly returned to their tasks.

Nice to meet you too, Maddox thought, unsurprised by the chilly reception. He was the competition, after all. And not only that, he was a low-down dirty deal-stealer on top of it.

"All right, people," Blayze announced, "four days to showtime. Get your workstations up and running." She left Maddox and Tommy standing in the entryway as she moved from person to person, checking their progress with shrewd, critical eyes. "I want to make a dry run in the test environment in an hour, so let's get moving."

Tommy elbowed Maddox. "What's she doing, boss?" he murmured. "Thought you were calling the shots on training up."

"That was the deal," Maddox said. Apparently, Blayze had other ideas. He lit a cigarette, blew smoke, and watched Blayze purposefully ignore him as she finished her rounds. Then she began setting up what Maddox gathered was her own workstation. Another minute passed and neither she nor the assembled crew acknowledged him or Tommy in any way. Not even a glance thrown in their direction.

I get the feeling you're not wanted here, boyo.

Thanks, Roon, I hadn't noticed.

His late mentor's voice haunted him less than it used to, but it never went away entirely. Maybe it never would, and that was fine with Maddox, even though he knew the voice was the creation of his own damaged psyche, a symptom of a wound that had never mended. Rooney was good company, dead or alive. And good company was hard to come by.

Maddox crossed the suite to the nearest youth, a kid maybe a year or two older than Tommy. The youth ignored Maddox, working away, his eyes fixed on a holo monitor, hands gesturing above his deck. The device's motion sensors detected the commands and presented a series of code blocks on the monitor. Maddox gave the images a critical glance. Security sniffers out of Berlin.

"I wouldn't use anything out of Germany right now," Maddox said. "All the best sniffers are out of Singapore these days."

The youth gave him an annoyed look, then looked beyond him.

"What do you think you're doing?" Blayze demanded from behind him. Maddox turned to face her.

"What your boss and I agreed to," he said.

She narrowed her eyes. "I don't care what you think your role is here, but I'm running the show. You're an extra set of hands on this gig, and that's it. We understand each other?"

He blew smoke. "All right," he said tiredly. "Let's go ahead and get this over with."

"Get what over with?"

"The pissing contest," he replied. "We could just call your boss and have him set you straight, or…"

"Or what?"

"Or I can show you why he brought me here."

She glared at him. "Show me how?"

A hint of a smile touched his lips. He lifted his chin at Tommy. "Kid, bring me a couple decks."

5
KICK

"Very bad idea, bruh." Tommy hovered over Maddox as the datajacker moved his hands through a series of command gestures, calibrating the deck to its new user. The suite's occupants crowded around them. Across the table, Blayze ran through the same gestures.

"She's wicked good," the kid warned, keeping his voice low so only Maddox could hear. "You saw how fast she trashed me last night."

"Trust me," Maddox said as he finished the setup. He reached for a trodeband, the shrinkwrap crinkling in his hands.

It had taken Blayze about two seconds to agree to the contest, the same kind of head-to-head challenge she'd bested Tommy in the night before. She reached up and enlarged her holo monitor, so Maddox could see the menu of simulated dataspheres.

"Same one from last night, old man?" she asked, swiping through the menu.

Maddox shrugged. "Your choice," he said. "Home field advantage."

She settled on a high-difficulty DS, one Maddox had never seen before. One she probably knew inside and out, which was fine with him. The more confidence she had, the better. And best of all, this particular simulation didn't require cloaking apps. The girl's selection had played right into his hands. Still, what he had in mind was far from a sure thing. Maybe Tommy was right to be worried.

Like a fighter staring down her opponent before the opening bell, Blayze scowled at Maddox as they both donned their trodebands.

"Let's go, Blayze," one of her companions said.

"Show the old-timer how we do it," another added.

An excited murmur filled the suite as the timer appeared and began its countdown.

Maddox took a deep breath, then gestured above the deck. The meat of his body and the room slipped away as his awareness plunged into virtual space. He became his avatar, floating in the dark void of the simulated environment. A couple dozen grid clicks beyond lay the challenge datasphere, a collection of pulsing, luminous geometrics, not unlike a cityscape when viewed from afar. A dense latticework of data streams connected the rectangular prisms and pyramids and cylinders, the visual representations of data partitions that corresponded to real-world organizational structures, usually company departments like finance, human resources, supply chain distribution, and so on. Uncountable bytes of information pulsed between partitions, transmissions through a cybernetic nervous system.

In the lower left of his perspective, a small window appeared, displaying his opponent's perspective, the same feed the crowd watched raptly on a large holo monitor. It was a standard setup for a datajacking face-off, each opponent having a view of the other's feed, and the spectators watching both feeds side by side.

What wasn't standard, and what no one except Maddox could see, was a second small window, which materialized on Maddox's lower right. The app catalog he'd loaded onto the deck from a fingertip archive moments earlier, the devious act hidden by a simple sleight-of-hand trick Rooney had taught him half a lifetime ago. As the timer began its ten-second countdown, he subvocalized a series of commands, fanning through the apps, pulling the ones he needed.

The audience chanted, "THREE…TWO…ONE…GO!!!" Applause and cheers broke out.

"Fuck him up!"

"You got this, Blayze!"

Instead of zooming toward the datasphere, Maddox orbited around it, scanning until he found his opponent's avatar. She was on the opposite side, streaking toward the DS like a missile. Damn, she was fast. He locked onto her and a yellow smiley face icon popped into view, a graphic that matched the face on the back of her jacket. Maddox's own icon was a disembodied hand flipping the bird. Seemed appropriate for the occasion.

He hand-gestured a command, then drew in a breath as his avatar thrust forward at blinding speed. He shot over the top of the DS and past it like a streaking meteorite.

The girl's crew laughed and teased him, misinterpreting the maneuver as accidental.

"You see that? He missed the whole thing."

"Hey, old man, you need some help? The DS is that giant glowing thing you just flew past." More laughter erupted.

Old man. Before today, he'd never been called that. It felt strange. He didn't think of himself as old. But then the label fit, didn't it? He was the oldest one in the suite by at least a decade. Thirty-two was old for a datajacker. Ancient, even.

He subvocalized, and his lock-on appeared, visualizing as a long green cord, connecting the two avatars. His display showed the girl's icon with a green circle around it, confirming the lock-on.

Nice to see you haven't forgotten everything I taught you, old man.

Very funny, Roon. Keep watching. You're going to love this.

Maddox's avatar settled in behind Blayze's as he followed her path.

"Hitching a ride?" the girl said, her voice a whisper in his ear.

"Don't mind, do you?"

The girl didn't pause, didn't slow down. She rocketed toward the DS, now looming bright and large before them. Maddox followed close behind her like a water-skier towed by a motorboat.

"Don't mind at all," she said. "However you want to lose is your business."

Maddox heard murmurs of confusion from the suite. The spectators' bewilderment at his tactic—at his *apparent* tactic—was hardly surprising.

Normally, following your opponent in a datajacking contest was anything but a winning strategy. It was the kind of thing rookies tried sometimes, when they lacked the confidence or experience to come up with their own plan for beating the simulation's puzzle. Fall in behind your opponent, watch where they went and what they did, replicate their tactics, and hope you could win the race to the finish line. Maddox had seen it work once or twice, but only when the winning competitor had screwed up, making some major mistake in the simulation's endgame. It wasn't likely that Blayze, who possessed obvious skill and no shortage of confidence, would make such a blunder.

The objective was a dataset locked away inside an archive, deep within the IT department's partition. The one who jacked the dataset and made it out of the DS first, undetected, would be declared the winner.

He stayed locked onto to her, watching as she called up a simple wire-cutter, the app visualizing as a pair of cartoon scissors. A moment later she'd cut a hole in the DS's outermost perimeter, a thin, semitransparent security barrier. Maddox admired her quick, neat technique, like a seasoned thief calmly snipping her way through a chain-link fence. As she passed through the gap, her smiley face avatar rotated around and stuck out its tongue at Maddox, prompting derisive laughs from her crew.

Cheeky little shit, he thought, though he was more amused than offended as he followed her through the opening. He stayed close, matching her pace as she slowed to a crawl, approaching the DS's core with prudent caution.

The geometry of the central cluster's partitions rose before them, a dense array of cylinders and cones and spheres. Each partition glowed and pulsed, all of them connected by weblike strands, the visual representation of the DS's interconnected data network. The strands thrummed, oscillating with the flow of huge amounts of information.

Maddox spotted the IT partition, a tall obsidian pyramid near the core. Blayze apparently spotted it too, rotating her avatar to face the pyramid and then heading straight for it. As they approached, Maddox still following, architectural details emerged. The simulation's creator had apparently been an admirer of ancient Egypt. At the base of the IT pyramid sat a pair of replica sphinxes, covered in a skin constantly shifting graffiti art. The pyramid itself had a smooth exterior, oily and black, with each of its triangular surfaces connected to its neighbor by a raised ridge filled with intricate carvings, indecipherable glyphs of some ancient language.

A collective gasp came from the suite as intelligent sentries, hundreds of them, blinked into existence on the pyramid's surface.

"Jesus," Tommy said, marveling at the sight. "You see that? Look at all of them."

They were kind of hard to miss. The sentries covered every visible surface of the pyramid. They visualized as scarab beetles, in keeping with the theme, scampering about, bumping into one another as they searched for intruders.

For the first time since plugging in, Maddox felt a stab of genuine worry. There were *so many*. It was like walking up to a hornet's nest someone had kicked a moment earlier, or suddenly realizing you were standing in the middle of a minefield.

Outside of a watchdog AI, intelligent sentries were among the most difficult security programs to deal with. The main problem was their adaptability. You could instruct ISes to do any number of wide-ranging activities. You could have them patrol a datasphere along a predetermined route, looking for specific threats. Or you could station them along known weak spots like a border guard watching for illegal crossers. If you preferred the hands-off approach, you could turn them on and set them free, letting their adaptive learning algorithms figure out where your DS's vulnerabilities were, and on their own they'd come up with strategies to shore them up or defend them.

On an actual job, you could take time to track IS behavior, get a feel for their operating parameters so you could come up with ways to fool them. But this wasn't a real job. In a face-off contest you didn't have the luxury of a long, ponderous preparation. In a face-off contest, time was the enemy. Whoever took longer lost. So you generally had two choices. You could take a quick-and-dirty scan and hoped it uncovered something useful, which took time. Or you could say fuck it and improvise, hoping your instincts and skill could get you through.

Blayze went with the fuck it strategy. Her avatar suddenly zoomed forward, straight for the hornet's nest.

Maddox followed. She was a cocky one, this kid.

As the next pair of minutes passed, Maddox realized he was wrong. Blayze wasn't cocky. She was, he corrected himself, but she wasn't *only* that. She was good. Impressively good. Far better than what he'd witnessed last night against Tommy. He stayed close to her, watching as she distracted a group of ISes with a cloned avatar, sending nearly half of the sentries chasing after a ghost and clearing a large section of the pyramid's outer wall in the process. What had she seen to make her think that might work? She might have been in this particular simulation before, or even many times, but the IS parameters were randomized with each session, so for her to distract so many on the fly was nothing short of remarkable. This Blayze had legit top-drawer skills.

He kept close, following her through the gap she opened up in the pyramid's shell. Once inside the partition, she took a quick scan and recalibrated her data profile to offset the partition's passive countermeasures. It was a move that disguised her from detection, like an art thief changing into a security guard's outfit after gaining access to a museum's inner corridors. Maddox did likewise, mimicking her every move, every adjustment.

"Boss, you can't just copycat the whole time," Tommy whispered, so close Maddox smelled curry on the kid's breath. "She'll leave you in the dust."

"Trust me," Maddox said, then turned his face away. "Jesus, Thai for breakfast?" The kid had to have an iron stomach.

Momentarily distracted, Maddox nearly lost track of Blayze's progress. She'd already found the target dataset and nicked it, prompting claps and hoots from her companions. Christ, how fast was she? Back in the suite, he felt his palms dampen with worry. Maybe his chosen strategy had been a poor one.

Too late to change it now, boyo.

I know, Roon, I know.

The dataset visualized, comically, as a cartoon bag of loot with a dollar sign icon. Blayze's smiley face avatar didn't waste time with snarky comments or taunting gestures, speeding past him with her bag of loot in tow. He chased after her, subvocalizing a command as soon as they exited the partition.

"What is that?" someone asked.

"What did he just pull out?" another voice said.

A moment later someone recognized the visualization, an old-fashioned police siren, rotating twin beams of light.

"It's a goddamn beacon!" one of the crew shouted.

The suite's onlookers murmured in confusion.

Speeding away from the pyramid, Maddox one-eightied his view, finding exactly what he'd expected but still unnerved by the sight of it. Alerted by the beacon, dozens of ISes detached themselves from the IT partition and shot straight for him. The prey had just waved a flag at the predators, daring them to chase after him…

…and after her too.

"The hell are you doing?" Blayze said in his ear. "You have any idea how fast those things are? If they get us both, I win."

"Is that what the rulebook says?" Maddox asked, even though like any datajacker he knew the generally accepted thinking. If they didn't get out clean, whoever had the target dataset in hand would be considered the winner.

"There isn't any rulebook, old-timer." The ISes had already cut the distance between pursuers and pursued by half. In another couple seconds they'd be on top of him.

"There isn't?"

"No, there isn't," she snapped.

"I'm glad you see it that way."

Under the table, he kicked her hard in the shin. The girl yelped in pain and Maddox heard fumbling, knocking noises, as if she'd fallen back in her chair.

In virtual space he accelerated and reached the smiley face, calling up the second app he'd smuggled in: a pickpocket executable. Appropriate to its stealthy nature, it didn't visualize as anything, visible only as a blurred smudge. The app made short work of the dataset, stealing it from Blayze like its real-world analog lifting a wallet from a distracted tourist. The app then loaded the stolen goods onto Maddox's temp storage.

From the suite, an eruption of cursing and accusations of cheating were hurled at him from the irate girl and her crew. Inside virtual space he placed the beacon on the girl's avatar and rocketed away from her milliseconds before the ISes reached them.

"You bastard!" she cried. "You cheating bastard!"

From a safe distance he watched her zigzag like mad, barking profanities as she tried in vain to outmaneuver the IS horde. It would only take a minute for her to remove the sticky beacon from her avatar, but they both knew she didn't have that long. Within seconds the ISes caught her, and Maddox watched with satisfaction as the smug little smiley face disappeared under a swarming attack.

A stunned silence fell over the suite as Maddox cruised leisurely past the outer security perimeter, carrying the dataset. A blinking checkerboard flag on the suite's monitor declared him the winner.

"Got to hand it to you, Blackburn," a voice said. "You've still got it."

Maddox removed his trodes, blinking as the suite materialized around him. Behind Blayze stood Dezmund, his hands coming together in a slow clap.

"A little devious," he said, "but well done."

"Thanks."

The girl ripped off her trodeband, furious. "He cheated!" She slammed the trodes on the table. "This is bullshit."

"There's no rulebook," Tommy said, happy to remind her. "You said it yourself."

The girl's face reddened, her lips pressed tightly together. She looked to her benefactor for support. "That was a dirty trick and you know it!"

"Yes, it was a dirty trick," Dezmund agreed. "It also worked, and that's all that matters." Then he spoke louder, to everyone. "And just so we're all clear on this," he announced, nodding to Maddox, "the old man's running the show on this one."

As the girl's features wavered between shock and humiliation, a small part of Maddox felt sorry for her. A very small part.

6
BLAYZE DOESN'T SERVE

The room fell silent as Blayze glared at Dezmund. Her peers shifted their anxious gazes between her and her benefactor, waiting for her reaction. An explosive tirade? A punch in his face? Quietly they stood, waiting but not knowing what was coming next, which suited Blayze fine. She liked being unpredictable. There was an advantage to that, to keeping people off-balance. Not that she was interested in what her ass-kissing half-talent peers might have been thinking at that moment. It was the old datajacker's reaction she was interested in, and she liked what she saw: smug satisfaction.

"Can I speak to you for a minute?" she hissed at Dezmund. She stood up quickly, knocking the chair backwards to the floor and stomping out of the room, slamming the door behind her.

*   *   *

A minute later, Dezmund and Blayze were alone in the suite at the end of the corridor. The one he'd rented just for the two of them, where no one else was allowed to enter.

"Christ, my leg hurts," Blayze said, locking the door. She bent over and rubbed her shin.

"You need some ice?" Dezmund asked.

She stood back up. "It's just a little bump. Tricky son of a bitch, your old buddy."

Dezmund grinned at her. "Not as tricky as you, though."

Two seconds alone and Dez was already kissing her ass, already settling into his rightful place.

"Made a good show for the old man, didn't I?" she said. "The little girl throwing a temper tantrum." The kick had actually been helpful in hindsight. The sharp pain had made her performance all the more convincing.

Her shin still throbbing, she strode across the room, knelt down and slid a large suitcase from under the bed. "I'm all wired up," she said, heaving the case on top of the bed and pressing her finger against the bio-reader. "I need you to help me relax." Latches unlocked with a click. She opened the lid, pulled out a black silk bag, and threw it at Dezmund.

He held the bag gingerly and stared at it, his expression unsure. "Right now?" he asked. "I…I'm not sure it's the right time—"

"Are you suddenly in charge of the schedule?" she interrupted.

He lowered his head like a good little bitch. "No, I'm not," he murmured. She felt a tiny stab of pleasure at his obedience. Then as he removed the cuffs from the bag and quietly held them out to her, she felt another.

A minute later she had him naked and spread-eagle, hands and feet bound and chained to anchors in the door frame she'd had installed the day before.

A black leather mask with eye and mouth holes and a built-in trodeband covered his head. If only his crew could see him now, she thought.

Across the bed lay an assortment of paddles, canes, clamps, gags, and coils of restraining rope. She reached for the nipple clamps, relishing his gasps and the way he winced as she attached them to his body.

"He bought it," she said, running a finger down the center hairline of his stomach. His nipples were flat and distended in the clamps. "You see the look on his face?" she said. "Maddox bought the whole thing, didn't he?"

"Yes, mistress," Dezmund whispered, careful not to raise his voice. Her little bitch knew better than to speak in anything but a deferential whisper. "You were very convincing."

She tugged lightly on the small chain connecting the clamps, eliciting a small groan from his little bitch mouth. "I thought so too," she said.

He muttered something so low she couldn't make it out.

"What was that?" she asked, tugging a bit harder on the chain.

"I said he's smart, though. We can't underestimate him. We've got to be careful."

"You have doubts?" she asked, still holding the chain, her face close to his. "Doubts about what we're doing? Doubts about me?"

"No, mistress," he insisted. "Not about you. I'm just worried this could backfire on us. I, ahhh…"

A stiff jerk on the chain silenced the little bitch. "Let me do the worrying, all right? Everything's going exactly to plan."

The head-to-head datajacking contest hadn't been

part of the plan, of course, but she'd found a way to make it work, to twist the unexpected challenge to their purpose. Dez had stupidly agreed to let the old jacker run the breach strategy, and she knew if she didn't push back, if she didn't play the resentful upstart, Maddox might become suspicious. Inside the simulation, once she'd felt the sharp pain in her leg, she'd known what Maddox was up to. So she'd played along, pushing backward in her chair and making a show of losing control, then throwing an irate fit in the aftermath. A pretty decent performance, in hindsight. And the old jacker's apparent victory, on her home turf and in front of her crew, had undoubtedly stoked the man's ego. That had been the icing on the cake. When men were impressed with themselves, they couldn't see clearly. They were much less likely to feel vulnerable. Right about now the old jacker was feeling exactly how she wanted him to feel: confident and powerful.

Pretty much the opposite of Dez at the moment, she mused inwardly as she released the tension on the chain, letting it dangle loosely. Her little bitch exhaled in relief.

"Forget about him," she said.

"Yes, mistress," Dez said, lowering his head further.

She ran her hand over a VS deck on an end table, gesturing up a menu. She swiped through scenarios until she found one that suited her mood. A second gesture loaded it. Dezmund drew in his breath as he plunged into his new reality. She moved over to him, watching him squirm and twitch.

"Besides," she said, "we couldn't back out even if we wanted to, right?" She reached out, grabbed him by the balls, and squeezed. "Right?" she repeated.

"Ah, ah!" he cried, though still managing to keep his voice low. "Yes, yes, yes, right, right. You're right."

She held him a bit longer, savoring his discomfort, then finally let go. He let out another long, relieved breath.

Stepping back, she ran her eyes over him with immense satisfaction. She had him under complete control. And not just here, but everywhere. Every business decision he made, every aspiring datajacker he hired or fired, every dollar he earned and spent, even every piece of furniture he selected for his condo. There wasn't a decision in Dezmund Parcell's life she didn't make for him. How masterfully she'd worked him, first getting his attention with her jacking skills so he'd hire her, then gaining his trust over time. He'd opened himself to her, and she'd played him like some musical instrument, tuning him and plucking his little bitch strings until he sang the way she wanted. The way he wanted, too, deep down. Some served, some ruled. It was the way of the world.

Her mother had served, taking countless men into her bedroom, day after day, year after year. She'd earned less in a year of turning tricks than Blayze made in one datajacking job. Her brothers and sisters had served too. Working long hours at shit jobs for a pittance, their lives hardly any better than some dolie layabout who sponged off the system. When you served, you always had a boot pressing down on your neck. You lived poor and died poorer. And you never saw life above the City floor. Blayze had promised herself long ago she'd never let herself end up like everyone else in her family. She'd find a way to be the one giving commands, not obeying them.

And she'd kept that promise. With patience and cunning, she'd installed herself as the invisible puppet master of the City's most prestigious crew. Unlike Dezmund, she didn't give a damn about the trappings of power, about infamy or the adoration of her dim-witted peers. She cared only about possessing power and wielding it. Which made theirs a perfectly symbiotic relationship. One was the private power, the other was the public face. One was the dom, the other was the sub. One ruled, one served.

"Now," she said, backing up a step, "tell me where you are."

Through the mouth hole, he licked his lips. "I'm in the middle of the street, naked. There's a crowd around me."

"And what are they doing?"

"They're pointing at me," he said, his voice shaking. "Laughing at me."

She unbuttoned her pants and slid her hand beneath her underwear. "Tell me again," she commanded. "And talk slow."

* * *

Blayze sat on the bed, propped up against the padded headboard, a pillow behind her head. Completely relaxed now, she let out a long, blissful breath. Her shirt hung on her loosely, and her bare legs were crossed at the ankles. Somewhere on the floor lay her discarded underwear. She'd find them in a minute.

God, she'd needed that. The small break from all the tension and stress had worked wonders. Her limbs felt loose and relaxed, her mind clear and unfettered by worry. You had to take care of yourself.

Because no one else would. She'd read that somewhere, in some book about successful, driven types. Or maybe she'd seen it on a feed. If you didn't have an escape from your troubles, if you didn't have something that could take your mind off things, you'd end up burned out or your health would suffer or you'd be eaten alive by your problems.

The chains attached to the door frame swayed back and forth. The bathroom door opened and Dez appeared, now fully dressed and holding the mask he'd been wearing until a few minutes ago.

He placed the mask on an end table. "I've got to get back in there."

"So do I," she said. "I'm right behind you." She smiled. "Just a couple more minutes of afterglow."

He returned the smile, awkwardly. It was the expression someone gave you when they didn't really share your happiness but didn't want to be impolite.

As always, he'd wanted to touch her and she hadn't let him. He'd never touched her before. She'd never allowed it. And she never would, of course. He had to know that by now, didn't he? Had to know the way he begged and begged to touch her, and the way she always refused, was part of the game. Right? He had to know she'd never get off under his touch, that the only hands capable of satisfying her were her own. Or maybe he only knew this on some subconscious level, and his conscious mind hadn't yet accepted it. If that was the case, she just had to be patient with him. He'd come around to her way of seeing things eventually. Come to accept her rules and boundaries. He always did.

"I'll see you down there," he said, then left the suite, closing the door behind him.

"Lock," she said, the command followed by the hiss-clack of bolts moving into position. Placing her feet on the floor, she slid off the bed and found her underwear hanging down the side of the ottoman. She reached for them. Playtime was over.

A minute later she sat at the suite's workstation in front of a holo screen, fingering a trodeband in her hand like a rosary. She had to call in. That had been part of the deal. She couldn't just skip it. Steeling herself, she slipped the trodes over her head, then gestured.

"Hello," she said. "Fine....I'm fine, thank you....Yes....Yes, everything's on schedule....Just as we agreed."

7
TRAINING THE CREW

Maddox floated high above the scene like a god, watching them. But not like the god the religious types went on about, that disinterested watchmaker who wound up the universe and let it go, who hoped his smart little monkeys chose him above all other distractions. No, this was something more like the old Greek gods, who pulled the strings of mortal lives without hesitation, who moved them around the board like pieces in a game, free will be damned. The avatars he watched, those glowing little orbs darting about the datasphere's luminous core, were doing exactly as he'd instructed them. The little orbs had come a long way in a short time, the god of virtual space noted with satisfaction.

It was the third and final day of prepping for the job, and the crew had almost finished their fourth dry run of the day. Maddox observed from a distance, hovering in empty VS. The simulated environment was an offline construct, identical in every way to the one they'd be running up against on the job. In every way *they knew about*, Maddox corrected himself. You could never simulate a datasphere entirely. Even with an insider feeding you specs like they had on this job, you never had perfect intelligence.

The crew was good. One of the best Maddox had ever seen. It was no wonder Dezmund was the top dog in the game these days. In less than five minutes, the orbs had moved beyond the DS's outer perimeter and penetrated three separate data partitions. All this without making the slightest blip on any of the security apps. The countermeasures hadn't detected them. The intelligent sentries hadn't spotted them. They were a pack of invisible sharks, stealthy and deadly, hunting their prey without leaving a single ripple in the water.

Boiled down to its simplest explanation, the drill was a game of hide-and-seek. Maddox had placed the target dataset somewhere in one of the partitions, and it was the crew's job to find it and extract it without being detected. And they had ten minutes to complete the task.

Maddox flipped back to the suite. He paced back and forth between the two rows of eggshell recliners where the young datajackers lay, their trodebands on, their hands gesturing above decks held by docking arms.

"Don't get distracted," he instructed them. "When you're close, when you think you've beaten everything the DS can throw at you, that's when you have to stay alert. It's easy to let it go to your head, to fool yourself into thinking you're too smart to get caught. Don't fall into that trap."

He reached Tommy's recliner at the end of the row. "You have to stay focused," Maddox said, reaching down and flicking the kid on the forehead.

"Bruh," the kid blurted, wincing.

A chime tinkled in Maddox's ear. The proximity alert he'd set. Someone was about to find the treasure he'd buried. He flipped back to VS.

Invisible to the crew, he hovered a couple clicks outside the Treasury Department, where he'd hidden the target dataset. The simulated DS was massive, its central cluster of data partitions towering over him like incandescent skyscrapers, pulsing with torrents of information. Adjusting his visual to see through Treasury's razorwall, he spied a hole slowly opening on the partition's outer layer. A moment later, the fissure grew large enough for one of the orbs to float through it.

Blayze, of course. Even without the name tag floating above her avatar, he would have known it was her. She operated with a confidence and skill inside VS that the others lacked. Not that the others were inexpert by any means. But she was different. She was in her element.

And right behind Blayze, following her through the opening, was Tommy. Maddox smiled inwardly. No dummy, this kid. He knew who to tag along with if he wanted to be among the first to find the prize.

"And just when you think the job is done," Maddox announced, "bad things can happen, and you better be ready for them."

He heard a chorus of groans from back in the suite as he subvocalized a command. Alarms blared and the entire DS began to flash red.

Throwing a spanner in the works. That was what Rooney used to call this kind of thing, back when they'd prep for jobs. The datajacker who'd taught Rooney his craft had been from Newcastle, and the expression had stuck with his apprentice. Maddox liked the sound of it more than *throwing in a monkey wrench*, the American version of the saying, so he too had adopted it. Throwing a spanner in the works when you were training kept you sharp, kept you from becoming overconfident. Weird shit could happen to you on a job, so weird shit had to be a part of your prep.

Maddox gestured up feeds from the recliners' bio-sensors, toggled through them. Blood pressures shot up, respiration rates surged.

"Forget about your meat sack," Maddox preached. "The meat always panics. The meat will always betray you. It'll make you do things you shouldn't, take shortcuts that'll get you tagged and frozen. You have to leave the meat behind. Let go of it, let your awareness sink into the virtual."

It was a thing easier said than done, he knew. The mere act of plugging into VS was something only a small fraction of the general population could do without their senses being overwhelmed. A datajacker's brain came with preternatural gifts others lacked. Neural pathways predisposed for virtual space the same way a gifted athlete's inborn hand-eye coordination predisposed them for professional-level cricket or tennis.

But even among those talented few who could handle the demands of VS, fewer still could completely leave behind the awareness of their physical selves. The meat was always there, and comfortingly so, the anchor of their consciousness, tethering them to reality. A flesh-and-blood security blanket, the meat was difficult to let go of entirely.

When Maddox checked Blayze's stats, he wasn't

surprised to find her pulse had hardly moved beyond normal. Every time he'd thrown a spanner in the works over the past few days, she'd been able to handle it brilliantly, keeping calm, staying on task. She alone among her peers had that special talent, that rare ability to leave the physical behind. It was the first time Maddox had seen anyone—outside of himself—achieve such complete immersion.

Impressed, he watched her avatar closely, keeping an eye on her activity feed. She remained composed and collected despite the systemwide alarms, despite being detected by the countermeasures. Maddox had set the timer for ten seconds. When the timer reached zero, anyone detected would be frozen. Not *really* frozen like you would be in an actual DS, your muscles rigid, your body helplessly wrested from your control. In a simulation, an unpleasant little shock through the recliner served as a substitute.

She called up an analytic bot, which visualized as a manga girl's head, its cartoon face smiling. "How can I help you today?" it asked in cheerful Japanese. As she subvocalized her reply, Blayze searched for the dataset. She found it a few seconds later, a loot bag icon hidden in the uppermost section of the partition, nearly obscured by a thick knot of data traffic. She loaded the dataset into her temp storage while she fed the bot different cloak configurations. Five seconds to go. Her companions, including Tommy, had already scattered, prudently exiting the DS at top speed rather than have the countermeasures freeze them and geotag them.

With less than three seconds on the counter, she found the right config and quickly made the changes to her cloak, disappearing from the countermeasures like a ghost vanishing into nothingness.

"Easy-peasy," she said, snapping her fingers, knowing her companions, already unplugged, were watching her.

She exited the partition to awed murmurs of approval. Cruising beyond the security perimeter, she made a show of exiting the DS at a leisurely, unhurried pace.

She's good, boyo.

No argument there, Roon. The kid knows what she's doing.

Kind of makes you wonder why they need you, doesn't it?

Maddox flipped back to the suite, Rooney's words echoing in his head as he removed his trodeband. Blayze had already unplugged, and she sat with her legs over the side of her egg recliner, smiling triumphantly. Clad in tiny shorts and a snug T-shirt, she slid off the recliner, bare feet pressing against the floor. Tommy's egg was next to hers; he and the others applauded as she did a little celebratory dance. She locked eyes with Tommy, her arms raised, hips wiggling, breasts teasingly close.

It was the more obvious of several intimacies Maddox had noticed between them over the last few days. Murmured conversations as they prepped their gear. Shared glances and secret smiles. He'd learned the two had grown up in the same hiverise, though they'd never met until their duel at Winner Take Nothing. Her sudden connection to him, however, had nothing to do with their shared background. She was clearly working the kid. And Tommy was either oblivious to it, or he knew and didn't mind. Maddox guessed it was the latter. As with most his age, enslaved to raging hormones, there were few things as mesmerizing as a pair of tits shaking in your face. Even when those tits had an agenda.

When he was alone with the kid later, he asked Tommy straight out. "She recruiting you?"

"Kind of," the kid said, his face reddening.

"What did she say?"

The kid avoided Maddox's eyes. "Just asking me how happy I was being the only jacker on your crew. If I ever thought about 'moving up.'"

Moving up. The words were at once an enticement to Tommy and a dig at Maddox. The devious little witch.

"And what did you tell her?"

Tommy shrugged. "Told her I was fine, but I'd call her if anything changed." He said it without conviction, almost defensively. Maddox believed him, but he also wondered if the kid was giving him some sanitized version of the truth. Maybe he hadn't been quite so definitive with Blayze.

It had to be tempting, of course. Big crew with a solid rep. And the eyelashes batted at him were surely persuasive. But he and Tommy went back, not a long way, but long enough to know they had each other's back. And for them, that kind of thing mattered. The same way it had mattered with him and Rooney.

Still, the kid was restless by nature, and he'd shown Maddox his ambition more than a few times over these last months. At some point Maddox knew the kid would want to leave. A two-man operation would be too small, too limited for the kid's aspirations. It seemed inevitable that day would come, sooner or later.

"So you think we're ready?" the kid asked, anxious to change the subject.

Maddox lit a cigarette. He looked beyond the kid, gazing around the suite. The young datajackers fiddled with their gear, ate noodles and mini burgers from carryout boxes, watched holo replays of their successful dry runs. Anticipation and excitement hung in the air, like the last few moments before a soccer match or a car race. Their engines were revving; they looked ready to go. Readier than he felt, but then he always felt that way, like he was never quite ready. Like he needed more time, more intel, more gear. Blackburn Maddox, the obsessive planner. Maybe that was why he was still alive, still out of jail. Probably was.

He blew smoke. They were good, these kids. He couldn't deny it, even as his worries, both the legitimate and the misplaced kind, tugged at him, trying to convince him otherwise. It was go time.

"Yeah, kid. I think we are."

8
GRAVEYARD SHIFT

"Come on," Boaz said, "you said you'd think about it."

"That's what you remember me saying," Iris answered. "But it's not what I said."

Boaz had been on her for a week about it. Wouldn't let it go. Iris knew working the graveyard shift would be different, but this wasn't exactly what she'd been expecting.

Everyone was expected to work the graveyard shift at some point. If you take your career at BNO Commerz seriously, her boss had said, then you'll work graveyard for a few months. Pay your dues, get a feel for how things work after hours, blah blah blah. And so when Marco and his partner had a baby and a slot opened up, she'd raised her hand and volunteered. Iris was a dedicated employee, after all. A company woman, a serious professional. So she always made sure to do what a good company woman would do.

The graveyard shift had its upsides, for sure. In the hours between midnight and dawn, BNO's data security department had a skeleton crew on hand, which meant her span of control was wider than it would be during normal business hours. She had access to more systems and had greater authority to make decisions. It was like being promoted, in a sense. More responsibility, more accountability. And they bumped her pay for working off-hours, which wasn't bad, either.

Aside from the boredom and the unnatural hour—three months in and Iris still hadn't adjusted to waking up at 7 p.m.—the biggest downside was Boaz, the only other datasec employee who worked the same shift at her location. Unlike Iris, he worked graveyard on a permanent basis. Also unlike Iris, he couldn't take a hint. Which could be frustrating.

But it was also useful.

The two of them occupied a pair of workstations in an otherwise empty control room. Four holo displays covered one wall, projections of the company's datasphere. The center pair toggled through visualizations of critical locations and partitions, like security cameras blinking through a building's hallways and parking garages. The outermost displays had dozens of performance metrics and statistics, pulsing and scrolling and blinking. All green. All good.

Boaz glanced over at the leftmost display. Something had caught his attention.

"What?" Iris asked. "You see something?" She felt a twinge of worry.

Her coworker shook his head. "No, just checking the hourly throughput."

"It's not updated yet," she said. "Ten more minutes." It was two fifty in the morning. The refreshed throughput figures wouldn't show on the display until three. On most nights Iris didn't watch the clock because it made the time pass more slowly. Tonight was different, though. She'd been obsessively checking the time every minute for the past hour.

"Oh, right," he said, frowning at the timepiece on his wrist. "This thing is an antique. You have to wind it up by hand. Keeps terrible time."

"Then why do you wear it?" Iris asked.

"I like it," he said, turning the little knob between his thumb and forefinger. "And Shasta gave it to me," he said with a wink.

Back to Shasta. Always back to Shasta. No matter which direction the conversation turned, all roads led back to Shasta and Boaz's obsession.

"She really likes you," he said, shifting the conversation back to his favorite topic.

"She said that?" Iris asked, glancing furtively at the time. Eight minutes until three. "Or is this you embellishing again?"

He put his hand over his heart. "Swear to God," he promised. "Her exact words were 'I think she's hot.'"

Iris pretended to mull this over for a long moment. "Even if I thought the same about her," she teased, "it doesn't mean she'd go through with it."

"But she would," he said quickly, edging forward in his chair. "We already talked about it."

"Bullshit."

"We totally did," Boaz assured her.

Again Iris acted as if she was considering it. Boaz leaned forward, devouring her with his eyes. Christ, how badly did he want to watch his girlfriend screw another woman?

Seven minutes to three. "And how do I know," Iris said slowly, "you won't be jealous?"

"I won't," he blurted, suddenly hopeful. "I won't, I won't, I promise."

Iris looked at him skeptically. "But we're coworkers. They always say you shouldn't crap where you eat, you know."

"You're going back to the day shift in a week, right?" he pointed out. "We'll hardly see each other after that."

She pressed her lips into a tight line. "I don't know."

"What's not to know?"

"It's one thing to say another woman's hot. That doesn't mean she'll do anything. You said she's never done something like this before. So how do you know she won't get cold feet?"

"She won't," he insisted. "I know she won't."

"Yeah, right." Five minutes to three. "In your dirty little fantasies she won't. Reality's different."

He removed his specs from his shirt collar. "No, really. She wants to. Take a look at this." He held out his lenses.

She looked at the lenses dubiously. "At what?"

"She wanted you to see some vids," he said, smiling naughtily. "Of us. She said I could show you. In fact, she wanted me to show you."

Iris hesitantly reached for the specs, narrowing her eyes at him. "She really wants me to see her?"

"She does," he said, all but drooling, the pathetic loser. "She's down for it, I'm telling you."

Iris turned the specs over in her hands. Three minutes to three.

"Not here," she said. "Not in the control room."

"Why not?"

"Because this is where I work," she said. "Because it feels weird in here."

Boaz's face dropped. Iris let him hang there on the brink of disappointment for a long moment. "The break room," she said finally.

"Sure," Boaz said, visibly relieved. "Break room. Go ahead."

"No," Iris said. "I want you to watch with me."

He glanced doubtfully up at the monitors. "But we're not supposed to…" His voice trailed off.

They weren't supposed to leave the control room. She knew it as well as he did. It was company policy. Strict company policy. A minimum of two badged employees—and only certified data engineers—had to be in the control room at all times. The company's datasphere had automated security in the form of intelligent sentries, secure razorwalls, and an array of the latest countermeasures, but human oversight and intervention were still vital to keeping things secure. Apps failed sometimes. False alarms happened. For all the advanced security a modern DS had, you still needed expert human eyes, ears, and problem-solving to manage the environment's complexity. Some companies farmed out DS management to AI service providers, but BNO preferred the human touch. BNO was old-school.

"I want you," Iris repeated, slower this time, "to watch with me." She fixed him with a fuck-me stare he wilted under so visibly, so completely that she almost felt sorry for him.

"Okay," he said, his face flushed. "But we can't be gone more than five minutes."

As he rose from his chair and turned, Iris slid her

finger across the surface of her workstation. A small gesture that went unnoticed by her coworker, it was the culmination of the longest con she'd ever been a part of.

It had taken months getting to that gesture. Infiltrating the company, the first step, had been the hardest part. But she'd interviewed well and they'd hired her, and from one day to the next she'd become Dezmund's plant in the operation, assuming the role of an entry-level employee. She'd eventually worked her way into the graveyard shift, where she had the access and opportunity to open a window into the DS, letting his crew slip in undetected. Months of acting, of pretending, of working the sex angle with Boaz so she could get him out of the control room for those critical handful of minutes. Boaz, as it turned out, had been the easiest part of the whole scam. Boaz was a sucker.

And suckers got played.

As they exited the control room, she donned her own specs and tapped a sequence on the frames, sending a tightly encrypted message.

WINDOW'S OPEN.

She checked the time. Two minutes to three, she noted with satisfaction. She'd told them the window would open around three o'clock, give or take a minute or two. Damn, she was good. Now all she had to do was watch some disgusting vids for five minutes, and then she'd walk out of the building and disappear into the City, leaving behind her short corporate career and an empty apartment rented under a false identity. And if the crew pulled off their end of the scam as well as she'd pulled off hers, in a few hours she'd be flush with cash.

And Boaz, pitiful sex-crazed Boaz, who walked beside her on their way to the break room, grabbing a handful of her ass, would end up catching more hell than any employee in BNO's history. He'd lose his job, and with his reputation shattered, he'd never find another job in data security.

And that would be the icing on the cake.

9
EXIT STRATEGY

"There it is," Dezmund said, pointing to a holo monitor floating above the suite's dining table. The words WINDOW'S OPEN flashed white and large.

"All right, people, ready up," Maddox said. The crew scrambled into action, climbing onto their eggshell recliners and firing up their gear. Some had giddy smiles. Others had no expressions at all, stone-faced and all business. Docking arms clicked into position, all holding identical Yakashima decks, loaded with apps specially modded for the job. About half the young datajackers had personalized their gear, adding stickers and custom shells. Blayze had a large yellow smiley face on hers, identical to the one on her jacket.

One by one, standby icons appeared above the decks. Maddox watched as everyone plugged in, and the standby icons blinked into connection symbols: a silhouetted head inside a green circle with waves emanating outward. Standbys took their places next to the recliners, one for each datajacker.

"Don't take your eyes off of them," Maddox told

the standbys. "You see the slightest twitch or if they sound like they're in pain, you yank off those trodes. Don't hesitate."

He turned to Dezmund. "Clock's ticking. Let's go."

Dezmund blew out a long breath and nodded. "Let's do it." Maddox had known him since the two were teenagers, and it was the first time he'd seen Dezmund this nervous. He'd almost bought into the idea that the man's vanity and ego were made of impenetrable stuff. And though Maddox had never cared for the man's showy self-absorption, right at that moment would have preferred the brash, confident version of Dezmund to this unsettled one. Self-doubt had a way of infecting a crew. A datasphere was full of dangers, even lethal ones, that could come out of nowhere at any time. If you let anxiety get the best of you, you were prone to hesitate or second-guess yourself, either of which could be disastrous. Virtual space was not a place for the timid or indecisive.

Maddox climbed into his recliner, pushing the negative thoughts from his mind, refusing to let his companion's worry become his own. Maddox wasn't superstitious by nature, but every datajacker knew it was bad luck to plug in if you lacked the confidence required to pull off the job. The Doubter's Curse, they called it. He reminded himself Dezmund didn't have a crucial role in the operation. He was there to help Maddox supervise, to keep an eye on things. They would be the two generals watching their troops from afar. So if Dezmund needed to sweat bullets to get him through the next ten minutes, so be it.

He glanced over at Blayze, lying on her recliner,

already plugged in and gesturing.

Kind of makes you wonder why they need you, doesn't it?

Rooney's words came back to him. As did the inkling about the gig, the notion something wasn't right. Nerves, he told himself. He always had nerves going in, even on small, uncomplicated jobs.

Never do a job unless you have more than one way out, boyo. You remember that, don't you?

Of course I do, Roon. That's one I never forget.

Gesturing his deck to life, Maddox's pulse quickened as he placed the trodeband around his head. His standby, a kid named Jonnie, took his position next to the recliner. As Maddox went to plug in, the kid grabbed his wrist, halting him in midgesture.

"Your smoke," the kid said.

Maddox looked at the cigarette still in his hand. Jesus, he'd forgotten it was there. The kid held out an ashtray, and Maddox took a long last drag, then rubbed it out. "Thanks."

He lay back and gestured above his deck, and the suite blinked away.

*   *   *

"You forgot your cigarette, seriously?" Dezmund needled him as soon as Maddox entered virtual space.

"Can we focus on the job, please?"

"I don't know, can we?"

"All right, all right, give me a break." Maddox said, unbothered by the taunt. "Got a lot on my mind at the moment." Good-natured takedowns, especially in stressful situations, were core to datajacking culture. His partner's disembodied voice, Maddox was relieved to hear, sounded free of the anxiety visible on the man's face moments before.

The two hovered in blank, unstructured space at their prearranged location on the public grid, far from BNO Commerz's datasphere. A few hundred grid clicks away, the company's DS was still massive despite the distance, not unlike the City's nighttime profile when viewed from inland New Jersey. Maddox had never seen such a large, complex cluster of data partitions. BNO's core business was banking, but its holding company owned an immense, diversified portfolio of enterprises. The company employed some two hundred thousand around the world, and its countless commercial arms touched nearly every industry. Agribusiness, genomics, construction, aerospace, asteroid mining. Whatever business you could name, more than likely BNO had a financial interest there.

A hundred grid clicks ahead of them, six avatar icons floated in two rows of three, speeding toward the datasphere. Maddox zoomed in, making out Blayze's smiley face avatar and Tommy's skull and crossbones. Moments later they reached the DS's outermost perimeter—the legal boundary separating public virtual space and the company's private DS, a felony-breaking point of no return datajackers referred to as "the fence."

"Calling up the CM," Dezmund said.

The command module app visualized around Maddox and Dezmund, flying into place like large tiles forming a three-sided wall around them. An array of virtual monitors and data feeds, the CM tracked the job's progress and vital statistics in real time. There were six HUDs, each labeled with a datajacker's handle, allowing Maddox and Dezmund to watch any of the crew's POV and activity feed.

Biometrics displayed for each jacker, supplied by sensors in the recliners: pulse rate, brain wave activity, and breaths per minute. The CM also showed data streams from scanner bots they'd placed outside the DS's perimeter days earlier. While the bots were too far away to track intelligent sentry routes or take samples of the razorwalls protecting data partitions, they were close enough to monitor overall DS activity levels—data traffic, application utility, user counts, and so on—by detecting small, almost imperceptible variations in the DS's visual signature. If Maddox and Dezmund were the generals in the command bunker, then the bots were their aerial reconnaissance, feeding them pictures of the battlefield.

The CM and the scanner bots, like Maddox and Dezmund and the rest of the crew, were concealed by cloaking apps, making the entire operation invisible to anyone except their own team, each of whom shared the same masking encryption. Had anyone plugged into the public grid where Maddox and Dezmund had set up their command module, they wouldn't have seen or detected anything but empty space.

Inside the DS, though, things would be different. Even with the best cloak, detection was inevitably a matter of time, mainly because of passive countermeasures. PCs permeated most dataspheres like airborne toxins, eating away at any unapproved tech. Originally created to keep a DS free of accidentally introduced viruses, their application as an anti-datajacker measure had soon become widespread. Passive countermeasures were found to be especially effective at dissolving the cloaking apps most jackers employed to hide their presence. In Maddox's time, neither side had yet claimed victory in this particular decades-long arms battle. When PCs evolved better, more effective algorithms, cloaking apps inevitably did the same. As the cat upped its game, so did the mouse. In practical terms, this meant that cloaking apps worked, and the best ones worked very well, but only to a point. Passive countermeasures would always melt a cloaking app, like an ice cube under a heating lamp. The thing was you never knew how long you really had: ten minutes or ten hours. It depended on how good your cloak was, how good the PCs were, and if the datajacking gods were smiling on you that day. Luck, as it did with most endeavors, played a large part. A DS administrator might happen to select a countermeasure configuration that closely matched your masking encryption, and your cloak would start dissolving the moment you got past the DS's fence. In those cases, if your plan involved staying inside the DS more than a few minutes, you were pretty much screwed. Aware of this risk, Maddox never planned a job to last more than ten minutes. Get in quick, grab your target, get out quick. That was how you had to play the game.

On this job, fortunately, he knew the likelihood of such bad luck was low. With months to plan and a mole employed at the company, Dezmund's crew had an insider's knowledge of nearly all BNO's security measures. They knew what digital weapons BNO had at its disposal and how it used them. Maddox couldn't remember when he'd gone into a job better prepared.

Still, you could never account for randomness. The bad luck lady got more datajackers busted—not to mention killed or brain-damaged—than anything else. You could have perfect information going in, and still an intelligent sentry might unexpectedly change its patrol route and run right into you. A razorwall might alter its security profile and detect you the exact moment you were cutting a hole through it. All security apps had random elements in their design, intentionally built into their systems. Stuff you couldn't plan for, only react to in the moment. And this was why Maddox believed he'd been brought on board. Dezmund knew his old colleague had seen and survived just about everything a DS could throw at you. And on this gig, the most important of his career—of both their careers—he'd wanted every advantage he could get.

"They're past the fence," Dezmund said.

Maddox checked the feeds. No cloaking app degradation yet. "Cloaks holding up," he said. "All six still at a hundred percent."

"Jesus, it's huge," Tommy gasped. In the kid's HUD, Maddox watched the DS grow, its crowded geometry of data partitions becoming larger and brighter.

"You're surprised?" Blayze chided. "It was huge in the simulations."

"Yeah," the kid said, "but that was, like, a game or something. This is the real deal."

With real danger, Maddox added inwardly. Keep your head in the game, kid.

As the six approached, details their offline function-over-form simulation had left out slowly began to emerge, design flourishes left behind by the DS's architect. Or rather architects, plural, Maddox corrected himself. BNO's digital self was too massive to have had any single creator. More likely, its current form had evolved, growing over time in waves of construction like some bustling virtual metropolis, each designer leaving stylistic fingerprints on their particular creations.

There were several manufacturing partitions, the largest and newest of which towered like a skyscraper deep within the DS's luminous core. On the partition's outer wall, abstract art, the kind that looked to Maddox's eye like spilled paint, faded in and out, making the illusion of a real-world building nearly complete. It was the kind of thing you saw often in the City, holo projections displayed on museum facades to promote art exhibits. Another partition—this one pyramid-shaped—rotated through video captures of BNO employees from around the world, visual clichés of its workers in scientific labs (white-coated Asian carefully examining a beaker with blue liquid), manufacturing facilities (Indian woman in sari and hard hat, flashing a thumbs-up), and business offices (sharply dressed corporati around a conference table, improbably smiling at each other). Maddox laughed inwardly at this last image of suit-and-tied executives with warm, friendly expressions. He'd lived the corporate life for a year and never once seen anything like that. A video of a dog brushing its own teeth would have been less absurd.

More details became visible. Razorwall facades with shifting honeycomb patterns. Spherical partitions of every color scattered about, their interiors cloudy and churning like magician's globes. A squat granite-colored cube topped with an ornate cupola, resembling some building from ancient Greece or Rome, the kind you saw on travel feeds with tourists going in and out. There seemed to be every design element Maddox had ever seen in a DS present in this single, enormous landscape. Cornices with gargoyles at the corners. Friezes with bas-reliefs of business icons: hands shaking, pie charts, stick figure businesspeople giving presentations and carrying briefcases. The sheer variety and number of shapes and colors and patterns was overwhelming. And between everything ran thousands of weblike filaments, the connective latticework carrying data throughout the company like pulses through a nervous system.

"We're about a minute from the target partition," Blayze said. "Cloaks still looking good."

Maddox confirmed the update, running his virtual eyes across the CM's multiple feeds. Everything green. Green was good. Green meant no alarms had been tripped, no intelligent sentries had spotted the crew.

In another minute the avatars would reach a small partition, the visualization of GloboEspaña, a fifty-employee entertainment network based in Madrid. The network's partition was notoriously fallible, as their inside connection had discovered, thanks to a local technical manager who resisted every corporate-mandated security standard until he personally tested it himself, which he rarely, if ever, seemed to get around to. As a very small fish in BNO's sea of companies, the Spaniard's pushback was largely ignored, a low-priority task that was perpetually the last open item on executive to-do lists. From a datajacker's standpoint, GloboEspaña's legacy security apps, left un-updated for years with well-known security bugs, were akin to a hole in the wall of a bank vault. A very tiny hole, to be sure, and one they never would have been able to find without the mole's guidance, but a hole all the same. And once they'd passed through, they could find their way through to BNO's corporate headquarters' partition, again thanks to their insider. With a slide of her hand across her workstation, the insider had kicked off a kill switch, temporarily disabling security protocols between the Spanish subsidiary and the headquarters' partition, opening a virtual door for the crew to pass through undetected. Once inside HQ, the infiltrators would locate the target dataset, dupe it, and then get out the same way they'd come in.

That was how it was supposed to work, anyway. Maddox felt his meat blow out a long breath back in the suite. Five layers of redundancy, he reminded himself. That ought to be enough to take care of any surprises. If Blayze's avatar glitched out or got frozen and she needed to unplug, they had five more jackers in line behind her, ready to take over the lead spot.

"It's hard, isn't it?" Dezmund said. "Watching and not being able to do anything." He must have sensed Maddox's unease.

"I don't know how you do it," Maddox commented. He'd always been a hands-on thief, always doing the job himself. This management-from-afar approach felt alien to him, even with all the prep he'd done. It managed to have all the stress and anxiety of a regular gig, but with none of the thrill of the action. No heady buzz of self-confidence, no addictive sense of his own invincibility, no sensation of being freed from the flesh and blood limits of his meat sack. Stationed far away in the CM, he experienced none of the things he enjoyed the most about his profession. It was like being some military drone pilot, stoically watching a battlefield feed from two thousand miles away, feeling none of the rush of combat.

The six avatars thinned out their formation, putting distance between themselves as they penetrated deeper into the DS. Clustered together, they'd run the risk of being taken out by a single defensive action, like a truckful of soldiers driving over a land mine.

Maddox checked their position. Half a minute out.

"So how much longer you plan on staying in the game?" Dezmund asked, using the personal feed only he and Maddox shared.

"What?" Maddox was caught off guard by the question. It wasn't exactly the best time for small talk.

"We're not young men, you know," Dezmund said. "At least not in our profession. You and me, we're ancient, my friend. Dinosaurs. I can count on one hand the jackers I know who made it past thirty without getting busted or brain-dead, and two of those fingers are you and me. Don't tell me you haven't thought about an exit strategy."

"Honestly, I hadn't given it much thought," Maddox answered truthfully. He'd been too busy lately worrying about his present. Pondering the future was a luxury he hadn't had time for. "You've got one, I take it?"

"You're looking at it."

"What? This gig?"

"Biggest payday I'll ever have. Enough to pack it up and call it quits. I've had my eye on a little beach house in Bermuda for a while now."

"Christ," Maddox grumbled. Dezmund hadn't mentioned this detail until now. Maddox had known the gig would be a lucrative one, but not *that* lucrative. "I knew I should have held out for more."

Dezmund laughed. "Tell you what, I'll let you stay at the beach house sometime."

"How generous of you," Maddox muttered. "So what, you're just going to bail on those kids?"

"Blayze can run things," Dezmund said. "She'll do just fine without me." Maddox caught what sounded like resentment in the man's voice. Lots more there, he gathered, but he didn't pursue it.

A proximity alert beeped in his ear. Blayze had reached the first marker, GloboEspaña's partition. And if the insider's information was accurate, she'd make quick work of the Spanish subsidiary's hopelessly outdated razorwall and breach the partition with ease.

"All right," Maddox said, switching to the crew's comm feed and pulling up the razorwall's config. "We're good on time, so there's no need to rush—"

Two of the crew flatlined. Maddox stared at the feeds in disbelief.

No way. It wasn't possible. Had to be a glitch. There'd hadn't been the slightest indication…

"Jesus H. Christ!" Tommy shouted in his ear, the kid's voice tweaked with panic.

"What is it, kid? I got nothing on my monitors."

"What the fuck is that thing?" another voice cried.

A shock of adrenaline shot through Maddox. Something had hit the crew, and hit them hard. Something huge. In the blink of an eye, the gig's priorities had changed. This was no longer a heist.

Now it was a scramble to get out alive.

10
BAILED ON

A flatline could mean one of two things. Either you were dead or you'd fallen off your egg recliner (or been yanked off, a third possibility) and disconnected from the unit's bio-sensors. In his early datajacking days, Maddox had once played a mean joke on his mentor while the two were plugged in, making a gurgling noise then sliding off his recliner. At the time Rooney hadn't thought it was very funny.

Maddox stared at the row of HUDs, trying to process what was happening. Two flatlines out of nowhere. But how?

"Tommy," he said, "we're going to get you out—"

"C-c-c-cold," the kid stammered. Something had hold of him, freezing him. Every panel in the CM erupted into flashing red. Warning sirens blared in Maddox's ears. A moment later he felt a strong chill pass through his own body. Whatever had Tommy was now reaching out across virtual space for him too.

"Standbys," Maddox groaned, the freezing pain already overwhelming him. "Pull us out. Pull all of us out now!"

He gritted his teeth against the cold and waited, but nothing happened. Then he realized he was alone in the CM. Dezmund was gone. They were all gone. Only he and Tommy were still plugged in.

Dread shot through him. They'd bailed on him!

His body back in the suite felt as if it weighed thousands of pounds. He was cold, freezing cold. Gathering his strength, he lifted his arm to his head. At least he thought he'd lifted it. He was so numb, so disconnected from his meat, he couldn't be sure if his body was obeying his commands. Working his fingers under the trodeband, he began to black out, his consciousness succumbing to whatever had his mind in its icy grip.

Then, in a jolt that felt like he'd hit the ground from a five-story fall, the suite materialized around him. He sat up in the recliner, breathing heavily, his clothes damp with sweat. In his gnarled, still-freezing hand dangled the trodeband. He tossed it to the floor.

Around him several recliners—including Dezmund's—were empty, rocking gently back and forth, abandoned only moments before. Four were still occupied: his, Tommy's, and two of Dezmund's crew, Renn and Jaylene.

His legs felt as if they were full of lead as he flopped them over the edge of the recliner. Pushing down on the edge, he lifted himself into a standing position, then hobbled over and yanked Tommy's trodes off. The kid's eyes shot open and he sat up quickly, shaking his hands as if he'd just pulled them out of a bucket of ice water.

"What the f-f-f-fuck?" he stammered. "What the fuck was that?"

Maddox shook his head. "I don't know. Something hit us."

The kid looked around the suite, confused.

"They bailed on us," Maddox explained, the cold finally beginning to ebb from his bones. He looked over at the two other occupied recliners. Renn and Jaylene lay motionless on the padding, their trodebands still in place. Neither of them was breathing.

Tommy looked at them with horror. "Are they…?"

Maddox checked them in turn, found no pulse on either. He shook his head. "They're gone."

"Are they the ones you…?"

"Yeah, they are," Maddox answered, averting his eyes from the bodies.

* * *

He'd have plenty of time to feel guilty about what had happened, but right now they needed to get out of there. As he helped the kid off the recliner, the light in the suite changed. In the corner of his eye, Maddox caught a police hover's red-and-blue strobe outside the window. In the quiet he could just make out the hover's engine whine as it floated beyond the thick glass. Then from the hallway came heavy footsteps and the clipped metallic murmurs of microphone-amplified voices. A sound profile Maddox had heard a thousand times in the hiverise of his youth. Rhino-armored cops.

"Come on," he urged, pulling Tommy toward the back of the suite, forcing his aching legs to run. As they scrambled into the dining room, the door in the front room burst into splinters. Rhino cops poured into the suite, their bulky arms brandishing automatic rifles.

"Closet," Maddox said, and they ran, sprinting into the suite's back bedroom and ducking into its large walk-in closet. Maddox removed an empty gear box from the back wall and began to stomp on the floor where the box had been sitting. On the third try the floor gave away, revealing a square-meter hole leading to the suite below. The escape route he'd cut out with a handsaw two days earlier, when he'd secretly rented the lower suite. It had been an act of caution bordering on paranoia, he'd thought at the time. He'd never imagined he might have to actually use it.

Tommy jumped down and Maddox followed, his weakened legs nearly giving out from the long drop down. They ran for the front door, the heavy thudding of rhino footsteps above their heads.

Maddox opened the door a crack, saw no one outside in the corridor, then signaled for Tommy to follow him. By the time the cops discovered the escape hole in the closet, Maddox and Tommy were five floors below, racing down the stairwell and then out an emergency exit on the ground floor. They donned their specs, toggling up a fresh set of fake IDs to fool the street cams, and lost themselves in the teeming crowd.

It was fifteen minutes before Tommy spoke again, the longest stretch Maddox could remember the kid had gone without saying a word. The kid was shaken to the core. Not that Maddox wasn't rattled himself, but he'd been on jobs that had ended in disaster before. This was the kid's first catastrophic fail. And what a nightmare of a first fail it had been.

"What happened?" the kid finally asked, keeping his voice low.

They knifed their way through the crowded walkways near Midtown. "I don't know," Maddox answered truthfully. "I've never seen anything hit a crew like that before."

"Was it an AI?"

"If it was," Maddox said, "it was the stealthiest one I've ever seen."

"There wasn't supposed to be an AI on this job," the kid said, his voice shaking. "That insider person said so. She said so."

"I don't know what it was. Could have been an AI or maybe just some new tech we've never run across before."

"But she said there wasn't one. She said it." The kid was babbling, still badly shaken up.

Maddox placed his hand on Tommy's shoulder. "Kid, calm down. We're all right. We made it out."

After a long moment, the kid muttered, "Not all of us did."

Though the kid hadn't meant to, the comment triggered a tremor of remorse inside Maddox. The two young datajackers had been sacrificed so he and Tommy could make it out. They'd taken the bullets meant for him and Tommy.

Maddox tried not to think about it as they passed under the red neon glare of Radio City. He blinked up an encrypted line and made a call, hoping she wouldn't reject the unknown ID he was using.

"Hello," Beatrice answered.

"Hi," Maddox said, then: "By any chance are you still in the City?"

11
SHOCK WAND RELIEF

Reina made a good living, doing what she did. And it was no wonder, Blayze reflected, watching her longtime friend and occasional lover perform her work. Reina was good at her job. Maybe as good as Blayze was at hers. At least on most nights, she thought sourly, thinking back on the disaster in BNO's datasphere a couple hours earlier.

"You're upset, I can tell," Reina said without looking over, her attention focused on the customer, gagged and stripped naked and spread eagle against the far wall, his wrists and ankles bound with intricate knots of white rope. Covering his eyes and ears were specialized specs, the kind used for gaming or, in this customer's case, sensory deprivation. The small, dimly lit space was empty of furnishings unless you counted sex benches and masturbation saddles.

"How bad was it?" Reina asked, reaching down and flicking the customer's plastic chastity cage with her fingernail, smiling at his helpless yelp. Her outfits varied, from traditional black leather dominatrix to barefoot surfer girl to Chanel-suited corporati.

Sometimes the customers chose, but most of the time she did. This particular early-morning customer, one of her longtime regulars, had a manga fetish, so she was the Japanese schoolgirl, sporting a plaid skirt with knee-high white socks and braided pigtails.

"I screwed up," Blayze confessed. The opaqued window began to glow with the first light of the day.

"Bad?" Reina asked, flicking the plastic cage again, harder this time. The customer gasped and begged her not to hurt him.

"Pretty bad."

Reina lifted an eyebrow. "Are we talking perfectionist disappointment bad, or cops raiding my parlor at any second looking for you kind of bad?"

"You don't have to worry," Blayze answered.

"I hope not," Reina said, then turned back to her work.

The sex parlor was off the grid, and as a favorite establishment of a highly placed police lieutenant, it enjoyed immunity from cop harassment. In the aftermath of her datajacking fiasco, it was the nearest safe spot Blayze could come up with, a place where she could duck out of public view for a few hours and gather her thoughts. She'd left Dez, still stunned and reeling from what had happened, down the hallway in Reina's office. She had no idea where her other crewmates had run off to.

Everything had happened so fast. Renn and Jaylene were dead. Dead and gone and it should have been Maddox instead. They'd all panicked, the entire crew, when things had gone sideways. Dezmund had been the first one out the door, which didn't surprise her. He'd been lukewarm on the whole thing from the beginning, so it had been no shock when he'd bailed first. But she was most surprised, and most disappointed, by the way she'd handled herself. You had to expect things to go wrong, and deal with them when they did. That was what a pro did, a real pro. Unplugging and hustling out of the suite hadn't been dealing with it. That had been panic, and now hours later, she was still raging at herself over it. Why the hell hadn't she taken a moment and slit Maddox's throat on her way out? He was there, still plugged in, as vulnerable as this poor sod Reina had tied up in knots. And what had she done instead? She'd run right past him like a frightened child. Fucking amateur hour.

"You look like you could spit nails right about now," Reina said, standing next to a table, opening a black case with brass clasps. She removed a meter-long rod that looked like an oversized magician's wand, then approached her friend.

The tip of the wand began to glow red, buzzing faintly with electricity. It was a shock wand, Blayze realized, a tool of Reina's trade. Same general design as a cop's shockstick, only with far lower voltage. Painful, yes, but a shock wand wouldn't make you collapse in a writhing fit or cause you to shit yourself like a cop's device would.

"Make sure you don't touch the hot end," Reina warned, then tilted her head toward the customer. "Go ahead, take over for a bit. You'll feel better after, I promise."

Blayze took the wand by the handle, felt its weight in her hand. She looked over at the customer, his pale, skinny body trembling. He looked around sixty, all saggy skin and white tufts of hair. "Who is he?" she asked.

"Does it matter?" Reina said. "He's a regular. Some highfloor corporati. One of those stressed-out, go go go types. Comes here twice a week before work."

Blayze stepped forward, gripping the wand's handle. She was still furious with herself, furious at what had gone down. What had she done to herself? To her livelihood? To her future? Everything she'd so carefully built up since she'd joined Dez's crew felt as if it were crumbling around her.

She reached out, touched the wand's glowing end to the man's belly. Sparks flew as he shrieked like a child and his body jerked. The smell of singed body hair filled the room.

Pleased and vaguely aroused by his reaction, Blayze felt her anger wane, losing a bit of its hold on her.

Damn, Reina really knew her stuff. This was exactly what she'd needed.

*   *   *

Half an hour later, calmed and once again in control of herself, Blayze sat across from Dezmund in Reina's office. The cramped space was tidy and organized, with no traces of their host's profession visible anywhere. Framed pictures of Reina's three children adorned the walls: a beach vacation, Disney World, primary school graduation.

"We fucked up," Dezmund said.

"We did," Blayze agreed. Then she asked, "How do you think he did it?"

"Had to be some kind of clone tag," Dezmund said. "They're not easy to make, and they're notorious for falling apart under a DS's countermeasures. But Maddox…" He sighed, shook his head. "He's good at that kind of thing. His builds are solid. Always have been."

Clone tags. Blayze had heard of them, of course, but she'd never seen one before. A clone tag was a kind of mask. That was the simplest way of thinking about it. Like people at a masquerade wearing the same outfit and the same disguise hiding their faces, impossible to distinguish from one another. Before they'd all plugged in, the devious old jacker must have secretly painted clone tags onto Renn and Jaylene's avatars. So when it came time for the killer app to do its job, it was suddenly faced with three identical Maddoxes instead of one. Determined to carry out its task, the app had resolved to take out all three targets. It had struck out at the nearest two first, hitting Blayze's crewmates with fatal brain spikes, killing them instantly and allowing Maddox a few precious moments to make his escape.

When the tech had lashed out at their own crew, Blayze and Dezmund had both jumped to the same panicked conclusion: they'd been double-crossed. In hindsight it seemed unlikely, but when two of your crewmates are murdered right next to you, sober reasoning pretty much goes out the window. Adrenaline and animal panic take over.

"You think Maddox knew something?" Blayze asked.

"No," Dezmund said, shaking his head. "There's no way."

"How can you be sure?"

"He was covering his ass, simple as that. He didn't take the gig at face value because he doesn't trust anyone, never has, outside of Old Man Rooney maybe. That's Maddox. That's who he is, and it's why he's lasted so long."

A part of Blayze wanted to grill Dezmund further. Give him a good tongue-lashing for not expecting the old jacker to pull some trick. For not finding the clone tags before they'd all plugged in. But then the larger part of her decided against it. Both she and Dez had checked and rechecked each jacker's gear, wares, and data signatures, including Maddox's. Truth be told, they'd both failed to find the old jacker's subterfuge. And what was done was done. They had other problems now.

She blew out a long breath. "So now we have to think about our next move."

"Hunker down," Dezmund said. "That's the next move."

"What are you talking about?"

"We just tried to kill him. That's all he knows right now. He doesn't know why, probably doesn't care why. We tried to kill him and we blew it. And so now he's got no choice but to come after us. That's how these things get worked out. Nobody forgives and forgets in this business. You start a war between jacking crews, and you're in it until one side wins and the other side is dead or run out of town." He paused. "And Maddox isn't the type to run out of town."

Blayze stared at Dez for a long moment, feeling some of her anger return. The little bitch had his head up his ass as usual. The mess they were in was far worse than some has-been datajacker's payback. And if Dezmund were as smart as he was vain, he would have seen as much by now. But he didn't, so she'd have to spell it out for him.

"Your old buddy might be a slick operator," she said, "but he's not the one we should be worried about. Not by a long shot."

12
JUST BECAUSE

Beatrice had been in the shower when the salaryman called and asked for a ride. He was in trouble again. When wasn't he? She'd stood there for a moment, letting the steaming water wash over her skin, as he'd waited for her response. He hadn't explained what had happened, what kind of mess he was in this time. He didn't seem to want to over the connection, saying only that he needed a ride and couldn't think of anyone else to call. Alarms had gone off inside her. Warning. Danger. Stay away from the salaryman's cage.

With a silent curse, she'd defied herself and dispatched her rented hover to go and pick them up.

What was it about this datajacker? He wasn't rich, wasn't connected. He wasn't bad looking, but neither was he head-turningly handsome. He was good in bed, but she'd had better. And he smoked. She so hated the smoking. Beatrice had had many lovers. Men, women. Most around her age, but a few much older and far younger. If asked, she could have pointed to something in each of them that had first attracted her. A sense of humor, a commanding presence, a flirtatious lilt in the voice, a pair of well-muscled legs. Beatrice had a thing for legs. But with Maddox, she didn't know what it was, why she felt so inclined to him, so connected. Even during their year apart, wholly out of contact with each other, she rarely went more than a day without thinking of him. Where he was. What he was doing. What kind of mess he was probably in.

Was it because they'd helped each other get through a life-or-death crisis? Maybe that explained it. The kind of bond soldiers had after going through some horrific firefight. A bond forged by an unlikely shared survival. Or maybe they were simply like souls. They'd both been born into poverty, and they'd both managed to use their respective talents to hustle a way out of it. Both saw the world for what it was, a teeming, chaotic mess populated by hunters and prey.

Or maybe it was something else. Something she couldn't name or put her finger on. Maybe she was simply a girl who liked this particular boy for reasons unknown, despite how much trouble he was or how many nasty cigarettes he smoked. For someone as fiercely independent, as wholly in control of every aspect of her life as Beatrice, her inability to solve this personal mystery was infuriating. For every other question in her life, she could find an answer, but for this particular why, the unsatisfactory explanation she finally, reluctantly, accepted was "just because." She refused to entertain the notion of love, of being in love. There was no place for love in a mercenary's life. So she'd settled on "just because" and left it at that. A mystery of the universe like those ancient lines in the Peruvian desert or the way a cat always manages to land on its feet. Some things you just couldn't explain.

In a terrycloth bathrobe with the hotel's logo sewn onto the pocket, Beatrice sat on the soft leather chair of her suite's living room. Her legs were crossed, and on her feet she wore matching terrycloth slippers, one of which she dangled loosely on her toes.

Sipping a cup of herbal tea, she said, "This is the part where I say 'I told you so.'"

Maddox and Tommy sat across from her on the sofa. The kid rocked back and forth nervously. Whatever hell they'd run into, it must have been pretty bad if the kid was still visibly shaken up over it. Tommy Park, former street punk and Anarchy Boy, might not have been around the block as many times as the suite's other two occupants, but he was no lightweight. She knew that from experience.

"I really ought to start charging you," she said, setting down her cup. "But something tells me you can't afford my rates."

Maddox went to light a cigarette. She considered stopping him, then thought better of it. The salaryman looked pretty hard hit as well. Not as much as the kid, but definitely out of sorts. A bit of nicotine in his system would soothe his jangled nerves.

"So what happened?" she asked.

Maddox walked her through it, recounting the job, how the crew had been jumped by some stealthy killer tech, how the standbys hadn't pulled him and Tommy out like they were supposed to.

"Maybe it wasn't a setup," she suggested. "Maybe you just ran into something they hadn't counted on, and they panicked." It happened. You never knew how someone might react in a crisis until the shit actually hit the fan. Some froze, others lost their shit. She'd seen that kind of thing plenty of times in her line of work.

"They were trying to take me out," Maddox insisted.

"Then their aim was pretty bad," she said.

"Actually, it wasn't," he said, explaining the precaution he'd secretly taken, the insurance measure only he and Tommy had known about. He called it a clone tag, then he described how it worked. Had Maddox not unplugged when he had, he would have been the killer tech's third victim.

"So you painted targets on their backs," she said. "Remind me not to plug in with you anytime soon."

Maddox sucked on his cigarette. "I didn't think I'd need it. Before we plugged in, when I tagged those avatars, the whole thing felt like overkill." He blew smoke.

"All right, then," Beatrice said, "so it was like I told you before. The whole thing was a sham. A way to get rid of you without looking like they did it themselves. From what you told me, your friend Dezmund craves attention like the politicians I work for. People like that, the kind who love being in the public eye, they hate bad publicity. They'll do anything to avoid it. And I mean anything."

Maddox nodded. He still looked a bit shell-shocked. "Yeah, that's pretty much Dez. I guess I should have listened to you."

Since she'd already said I told you so, she didn't repeat it now. And from the look on his face, not to mention the regret in his tone, it was clear he knew he'd messed up.

"Well, you both made it out of there in one piece,"

she said. "That's all that matters."

The salaryman smoked. "Yeah, there's that." Then he turned to the kid. "She say anything to you?"

"Who?" Tommy asked.

"Your little girlfriend back there."

"Like what?"

"I don't know. You two were looking pretty cozy the last couple days."

"What's that supposed to mean?" the kid said, offended.

"You tell me," Maddox said. "She say anything strange about the gig? Drop any hints you forgot to tell me about?"

"The fuck, bruh?" Tommy protested. "You think I knew something going in? She didn't tell me jack. And if she did, I would have said something."

"You sure about that?"

The kid shot up to his feet, his face red and contorted with rage. "You think…? You think I'd…?" Too worked up to get the full sentence out, the kid turned and stomped off into the kitchen.

"Jesus, salaryman," Beatrice said. "That was a bit below the belt, wasn't it? That kid wouldn't sell you out in a million years."

Maddox let out a long, tired breath. "I know, I know."

He started to rise up and follow after the kid, but Beatrice put a hand on his forearm. "Let him cool off," she said. "Poor kid's head is still spinning."

The datajacker seemed to agree. He sat back down, let out another long breath, and ran his hand through his hair. "That makes two of us."

* * *

While Maddox and Tommy got a few hours of

much-needed sleep, Beatrice hit the hotel gym and then shopped for clothes in the underground retail center near the hotel. When she returned, she called room service and ordered a late breakfast. Tommy, rested and no longer pouting, devoured a three-egg omelet. Youth, Beatrice reflected. How fast they bounce back. Maddox, still looking a bit ragged, scanned the police feeds in his specs, the same as he'd done when he'd first arrived at the suite. Again, he found nothing about him or any mention of a breach at BNO. It was as if the whole thing had never happened.

"At least the cops aren't after us," Maddox told her, removing his lenses and taking a seat at the dining table.

"You sure about that?" Beatrice asked.

He nodded. "When you've done this kind of thing as long as I have, you know how to read the signs." He buttered a slice of toasted bread.

"Silver lining," Beatrice commented. "So what now?"

Maddox didn't answer immediately. He glanced over at Tommy. The kid stopped chewing and stared expectantly back at the salaryman.

"I have to take him out," Maddox said grimly.

"Fucking right," Tommy agreed, biting into a sausage link.

Beatrice was afraid Maddox was going to say that. Afraid because in that kind of business, the salaryman was out of his depth. He was a thief, not an assassin. If you needed to steal intellectual property or cripple a rival's datasphere, Blackburn Maddox was your man. But killing was definitely not his bag. She didn't think he even owned a gun.

"Not really your forte, that kind of thing," she said, voicing her thoughts.

He shrugged. "It's not, but what choice do I have? Dezmund and his little wench won't stop coming after me now. They botched it the first time, and now they'll be worried about me coming after them."

So now it was kill or be killed, in other words. "What about kissing and making up?" she suggested. "Is that totally out of the question?"

Tommy laughed. "You kidding, mama? You can't lay down like a dog when somebody tries to take you out. I thought you were street, lady."

"Eat your breakfast," she scolded. "I wasn't asking you." Then to Maddox: "Well?"

He said nothing, only shaking his head. There was a grim determined look on his face she'd seen once before: when he'd learned a killer AI had murdered his friend. Maddox wasn't going to try and make peace, and he wasn't going to leave the City. He was going to take care of this bloody business once and for all, and she knew there was little chance of talking him out of it.

* * *

Beatrice rescheduled her outbound flight for the following day, and Maddox and the kid stayed in the suite that night. Maybe he'd change his mind about things before she had to leave. Men were more open to suggestion after sex. Sure, it was a lame manipulation, but she justified it by telling herself she might be saving his life.

She lay on her side facing him in the dark as he smoked a postcoital cigarette, a concession she'd reluctantly made to keep him in a relaxed state of mind. She'd practiced saying the words to him in her head, but now that the time had come, she knew they'd come out awkward anyway. She'd asked him this same question once before, and he'd said no. Would it sound needy or weak, asking him a second time? Or would anything like that even cross his mind? He was in trouble, after all, and he was unlikely to see her offer as anything but a way out of it.

Oh, screw it. Stop overthinking it and ask him already.

"Why don't you go with me?" she said, her hand on his chest.

The question hung in the air for a while. "I can't leave the City," he finally said. "Not now."

"Why not? I can get you a passport in a few hours. The kid too. We can be out of here by noon. Leave all this mess behind."

"This mess is my life."

"It doesn't have to be," she suggested.

He blew smoke. "What would I do with myself anywhere else? Jacking's the only thing I know, and the big jacking jobs are here."

"How old are you, Blackburn?" It was the first time she'd used his first name in a long time.

"Thirty-two," he said.

"Outside of Rooney, how many datajackers do you know who've made it past your age without dying or getting thrown in jail?"

He didn't answer for a moment. "None, but I'm the most careful one I know. So maybe I'll set a record."

"Be serious," she said. "You can't do this forever. You're lucky you've made it this far. Tell me I'm wrong."

He didn't say anything to that. She knew he couldn't. They both knew the datajacking game was anything but a long-term career. Even the most prudent, risk-averse jackers rarely had careers spanning more than a decade. Technology changed too quickly. You couldn't possibly keep current on everything. And the longer you stayed in the game, the more the odds stacked against you.

He broke her gaze and stared up at the ceiling. "I tried the straight life, remember? Didn't work for me." He tapped his cigarette over the nightstand ashtray. "I'm sorry, I can't go with you. Not now, at least. I've got to take care of this."

They didn't speak for a long time. She thought about leaving it there. He wasn't coming with her, and he seemed stubbornly resolved to his fate. Screw him, a voice inside of her said. If he wants to march down suicide road, let him. But then the moment passed, and the greater part of her realized she didn't want to be sitting in her home twenty-four hours from now, regretting things left unsaid.

"That chip on your shoulder," she said. "It's going to be the end of you, you know."

"What are you talking about?"

"That stuff you've been carrying around since Rooney died. Guilt or mourning or anger or whatever it is that keeps you from…"

"From what?" he said.

She clasped his chin and turned his face to hers. "From a lot of things." Then she added, "From me."

Flustered, he pulled away and ran an anxious hand through his hair.

"Have you ever considered," she said, "that maybe he wasn't the only one you could ever trust?" Her words came out all wrong, sounding more like a reproach than she'd intended. Christ, she was terrible at this kind of thing.

He reached over and stubbed out his cigarette. "I'm exhausted, Bea. I need some sleep." He turned his back to her and laid his head on the pillow.

She watched him for a while, until his breathing slowed down and she was sure he was asleep. Reaching out, she gently stroked his hair. Maybe he'd think differently in the morning, once he'd rested up.

Or maybe that was just her foolish hope.

13
LIES

Early the next morning Maddox stood next to the bed. Beatrice was still asleep, breathing slow and deep, her face half-obscured by her pillow. The sun wasn't up yet, and the dim light filtering in from the opaqued window fell over her features. Her nose was a little crooked. The shadow's angle, he noticed, changed halfway from the bridge to the tip. A tiny variation, barely noticeable unless you looked closely. Had she broken it at some point? Or maybe it had always been that way, and somewhere there was a mother or a father with the same nose? This new small detail reminded him how little he knew about her past. There was a whole lifetime of stories that was still a mystery to him. Her childhood had been poor like his, that much he knew. But had it been a happy one? Had she been the local tough of her floor, beating up all the boys? Did she have brothers and sisters? Had a lover ever left her high and dry? Had she been monogamous? Did she carry a burden with her, some dark secret that might surprise him?

So many things he didn't know. So many things he

wanted to know.

She's a good one, boyo.

I know, Roon. I know. But it's not that simple.

Or *was* it that simple? People did that sort of thing all the time, didn't they? Ran off together. Settled down. Had kids. Got a dog. Maybe it *was* a simple thing, just something he couldn't do. A kind of flexibility most possessed, but he simply couldn't bend that way.

And like he'd told her, what would he do with himself outside the City? He pictured himself disappearing, fading more and more the further away he traveled. Was it childish to think he couldn't live anywhere else? Was it simply anticipated homesickness? Or was the feeling spot-on, and he was such a creature of the City's canyons and superstructures that he was incapable of living anywhere else? Like some salamander adapted to live in only one ecosystem. If you removed it, it couldn't survive.

He moved to the window, gestured it a little more transparent. The view of the City from this height, at this hour, was really something. The kind of image advertised for tourists. The first touches of dawn kissed the mountain range of hiverises, their facades reflecting a warm, golden glow. Hover traffic zipped briskly along the stacked transit lanes. No slow-moving knots at this early hour. Far below, walkways churned with a thick flow of pedestrians, a multicolored river illuminated by holo ads like water reflecting light. The blues and reds and greens of early morning. Towering coffee mugs. Donuts. Noodle cups. A drama feed star peddling some "European hangover cure" packaged in tiny single-swallow bottles. That was a new one.

He darkened the window again. Beatrice still slept. He padded to the bathroom and slid the door shut. Opening the tap, he splashed water on his face. He looked at his reflection in the mirror as he dried his cheeks with a towel.

"I hardly know her, Roon," he whispered, but the ghost in his head didn't answer.

This business with Dezmund. It was no small thing. And though Beatrice believed otherwise, Maddox didn't think leaving the City would be enough to resolve it. If Dezmund really wanted him out of the picture, geography wouldn't matter. Living abroad, Maddox might be harder to find, but not impossibly so. And the idea of living in a strange new land, constantly looking over his shoulder, was less than appealing.

But there was more to it than that. If he ran out of the City like a dog with his tail between his legs, he'd never be able to live with himself. He wouldn't go out that way. Beatrice would laugh at such a notion, no doubt. Street bullshit, she'd say. Cred and rep and all that junk. Whatever he thought they mattered on the City's streets, beyond them those notions were meaningless. Currency with no value.

And maybe that was true. Probably was. Still, that didn't mean he could leave it all behind like it meant nothing. Like it wasn't part of him. He had to settle things first. Then maybe after that, when his accounts were balanced again, he could think about taking a different path. But not now. Not while he was hunted.

A hotel robe hung from a hook in the door. He put it on, padded into the bedroom, and fished his cigarettes out of the nightstand, careful not to wake up Beatrice. Heading out for a smoke on the balcony, he found Tommy seated in the kitchen, finishing a plate of leftover noodles from last night's dinner.

"She still asleep?" the kid whispered.

"Yeah," Maddox said. He pressed the button on the coffeemaker.

The kid slurped up the last of his noodles. "I was just leaving."

"Okay." Maddox removed a cigarette from his case. "Sure you have enough cash?"

"Yep."

"Want to go over everything again?"

Tommy gave him a cold look. "It's not exactly complicated."

The kid had a point. The plan they'd discussed while Beatrice had been shopping wasn't complicated. Still, Maddox thought he caught something else, something beyond curt teenage annoyance. Like the kid still was still pissed at him, still hurt and resentful from yesterday's harsh exchange, when Maddox had doubted Tommy's loyalty. He knew the kid thought of him as more than a crew boss and mentor. Questioning their bond, their friendship, had stung the kid deeply, more than Maddox probably understood, he admitted inwardly. He knew if Rooney had done the same to him once upon a time, it would have crushed him.

They sat there at the breakfast table. Maddox drank coffee and tried to think of something to say, something that would lessen the uneasiness between them. He wasn't good at that sort of thing, so they sat there quietly for a while.

"All right, then," Tommy finally said, standing up.

"I'm out of here."

Was it Maddox's imagination or was Tommy taller now? No, of course he was taller. At fifteen you were still growing. And Tommy was the picture of fifteen, all elbows and knees, that scrawny neck and bulging Adam's apple. Even in the new, fashionably adult outfit Beatrice had bought for him yesterday—a smart sport coat with matching trousers—he was still unmistakably adolescent.

Tommy lifted his chin at Maddox, the curt wordless gesture the kid used for both hello and goodbye. Then he threw a satchel (also a gift from Beatrice) over his shoulder and left the suite, quietly shutting the door behind him.

* * *

Minutes later Maddox sat on the balcony in the chilled early-morning air. He recalled his own balcony from his corporate days at Latour-Fisher, the tiny wedge of concrete jutting out from his condo, barely large enough to fit one person. This one was five times that size, with a large wrought-iron table and cushioned chairs. He leaned back in the soft padding and took a long draw on his cigarette. The sounds of the City were muted this high up, a distant hum punctuated by the occasional police siren. Even the transit lanes were quiet, the telltale turbofan whine subdued thanks to noise dampeners embedded in the balcony's three-sided enclosure.

He should have said something to the kid. Why hadn't he said something?

"Don't we look comfortable?"

Maddox started at Beatrice's voice behind him. He turned and saw her in the doorway in her tank top and boxers. "You could fit my whole apartment out here," he said.

"The Trade Minister likes to travel in style," she said, stepping outside. "When the general public picks up the tab, these highfloor government types never look twice at the price tag."

"It's a crime," he said.

She sat next to him. "And crime pays, doesn't it, salaryman?"

"Sometimes it does."

She crossed her arms, rubbing her bare shoulders. "Cold out here."

"A cigarette will warm you right up," he said.

"Right," she snorted. "I'll take tea, thank you very much."

He started to get up. "I'll have the bot heat up some—"

She grabbed his arm. "It can wait," she said, and he sat back down. She took in a small breath, like she was about to speak, but then didn't say anything. He knew what she'd been about to ask him.

"I didn't change my mind," he said. "I need to stay here and take care of things."

She nodded, seeming disappointed but not surprised. "I want to take the kid with me," she said. "There's no reason he has to be mixed up in all of this."

"He's not here."

She sat up straight. "What? Where is he?"

"On his way to a safe house," Maddox lied. "He just left."

She clearly didn't like his answer. "You let him go, alone?"

"He knows how to take care of himself."

"What if he goes and tries to get some payback on

his own? You know how he is."

"He's not stupid," Maddox said. "He knows that would be suicide."

Beatrice removed the specs hanging on her shirt collar and put them on. He could see her pulling up her reservation on the lens.

"What are you doing?" he asked.

"Changing my reservation again," she said.

"I thought you had a job to get back to." She'd told him as much last night. She'd also mentioned that her Canadian employer, the regular corporate gig that made up most of her income, hadn't been very happy about her delayed return.

"I do," she said, "but it can wait. Safe house or not, I'm not going to leave him here with a target on his back. I'm taking him with me."

He reached out and removed her specs.

"Hey!" she blurted.

"Didn't you tell me employer was pissed you were going to be late?"

"They were, but—"

"But nothing," Maddox interrupted. "You push back your date again and they might drop you. Don't give them a reason to go with someone else."

"It's a job, salaryman. There are lots of others out there."

"Look," Maddox said, "you told me it's a good gig, yeah?"

She shrugged. "Sure."

"Pays well?"

"It does."

"Then there's no reason to screw it up, is there?" Before she could protest again, he said, "Look, I'll put the kid on a plane and send him to you tomorrow, all right? Maybe it is better that he's out of the City. I was going to catch up with him at the safe house after you left. I'll send him your way tomorrow. Nothing's going to happen to him in the next few hours."

She narrowed her eyes at him. "You'll keep him out of it?"

"Yeah."

"And you'll send him right to me?"

"I will."

"Promise me," she said.

"I promise."

She turned it over for a while, then finally nodded. "Okay, salaryman."

She stood and went back inside. A moment later he heard the faint spray of water from the shower.

As he twisted out his cigarette in the ashtray, the second-guessing began. He'd told many lies in his life. Big ones, small ones. He'd lied to friends, lovers, cops, clients, even to Rooney on occasion. He couldn't remember any of them unsettling him as much as the ones he'd just told Beatrice. But he'd had to do it. If she knew the truth, she wouldn't leave. It was for her own good. She had a life to get back to. A good life. But the more he told himself that, the more it sounded like...like he was lying to himself as much as he was lying to her.

14

NEW FULTON

There was only one hiverise in Hunts Point, a small peninsula jutting out from the South Bronx into the East River, and its name was New Fulton. Home to over a hundred thousand, New Fulton was referred to by most of its residents as simply NF, an abbreviation that took on a variety of pseudonyms. The young frequently used Not Fun. Teenage boys who couldn't get laid called it No Fucking. On the ground floor there was a mystic who read tarot cards, an old woman who called the place Never Forever.

Most of the City's hiverises had come into being over the last century. Standalone buildings of the previous era had slowly grown into one another, daisy-chained into huge megastructures connected by hundreds of improvised tunnels and corridors. Over time ten, twenty, or more standalones might come together, like the fused vertebrae of some enormous creature, forming the self-contained worlds referred to as hiverises, each with its own unique identity. NF was the rare breed of hiverise that had grown out of a single building: the New Fulton Fish Market. A warehouse-like structure of some 400,000 square feet sitting on the tip of Hunts Point, the original facility had once housed one of the world's largest seafood wholesaler operations. The long high-ceilinged building had once been filled with iced pallets of tuna and lobster and crab, teeming with busy buyers and sellers and forklift drivers. That era was long gone, an artifact of the past that now only existed in historical feeds and library archives. The fish market had long since been subdivided into thousands of tiny residential units, food kiosks, and merchant stalls. Over time the building had tripled in size, growing haphazardly upward and outward, its irregular roof reaching six stories (seven in some parts) and topped with chimney-like projections sprouting skyward several more stories. The residents called these projections "the Towers," where the rich—or rather, rich by a hiverise's impoverished standards—made their homes. Local crime bosses and slumlords, for the most part.

As he made his way down Halleck Street, Tommy's old stomping grounds slowly rose into view. NF. No Fucking. Never Forever. His birthplace. The crowded, teeming hiverise he'd called home for most of his fifteen years. Tommy Park's turf.

He knew its real name, of course, but like everyone else he rarely used it. It struck him as absurd that such an ancient dump had the word "new" as part of its name. He'd noticed that about the hiverises in Manhattan, too, how the names often had nothing to do with the place itself. Like the ones called Paradise or Supreme or The Royal Arms. He'd been to Paradise and it was anything but, and Supreme was about as sketchy and low-rent as anywhere in the City. He'd never visited The Royal Arms, but from its name alone he was sure it had to be a royal dump.

The East River was hidden by the looming seawall just beyond the hiverise, but he could hear the churn of its high tide, feel its wetness in the air. He could smell it, too, its briny stench hitting his nose. It smelled like home, and it triggered a memory of the first time he'd actually seen the river. He was ten years old, and he'd finally summoned the courage to scale up the face of the seawall. He'd been the first of his playmates to make the perilous five-story climb up the old workers' scaffold, an ancient rusted-out framework, more of it missing than there. When he'd reached the top, he'd flexed like a pro wrestler to his turfies far below and dared them to do what he'd done.

How long had it been since his last visit to NF? A couple years? Three? The place really looked different now. What had changed? It was the roof. Yes, that was it. Another tower had been added on the west end. Maybe a new syndicate boss had moved in. He'd have to ask his turfies about that.

But it wasn't only the roof's profile that struck him as different, as changed from his memories. The place looked smaller now too. It was strange to think of a hiverise as small. No hiverise was small. But still, that was the vibe the place gave him. It also felt safe, and this struck him as even more laughable than thinking of it as small. NF wasn't anywhere near safe, never had been. Maybe it seemed that way because of all the hell he'd gone through since he'd left here. Like the way a filter app in your specs changed the way you saw things. Maybe that was what was happening now.

Or maybe it was the other way around. He'd grown up with a filter in place, and only now was he seeing things without it. He laughed inwardly at his own thoughts. He sounded like some cheesy head shrinker on the self-help feeds.

He spied the old radio tower, a makeshift aluminum frame erected decades ago by some pirate broadcaster. Tommy used to climb up to the tiny landing near the top, barely large enough to sit on, and watch the sun disappear into the City's great canyons. He'd dream of one day leaving NF and making his mark as a data thief.

Reaching the end of Halleck Street, he stepped onto what was once the fish market's parking lot, now a flat expanse of undergrowth that had slowly reclaimed the space, creeping out of gaping cracks in the ancient concrete. He stopped suddenly, hearing something. A faint buzz at first, the sound grew steadily louder. A motorbike's engine.

Tommy smiled. He couldn't see them yet, but he knew what he was hearing. He picked out three—no, four motors. In the next moment he saw the first Anarchy Boy, a streak of red tearing around the side of the hiverise. Jaybird. Even at a distance, the way he leaned over the gas tank was unmistakable. Tommy had once told Jaybird he looked like he was constipated, the way he was always hunched up with his ass sticking out.

Three more riders appeared. Z Dog, Girlie, and Snatcher. Z Dog still had the green mohawk, but it was a bit longer now, flapping behind him like a flag in a strong wind. The four riders converged on him and hopped off their bikes.

"Bruuuh!" Z Dog cried, punching Tommy's

shoulder. "Good to see you back on the turf."

"Tommy Thai," Snatcher said, grinning, using the old nickname. Tommy's heritage was Korean, but he'd earned the moniker from his insatiable love for Thai noodles. His turfies had known him to eat nothing else for stretches of days.

"What are you doing back here, TT?" Girlie asked. "Trying to get us in trouble again?" she joked.

"Nah," Tommy said. "Nothing like that, G." He couldn't help noticing Girlie's skinny, boyish frame had changed since the last time he'd seen her. She had curves now. Good ones.

"I'm up here," she said, pointing to her face. Tommy felt his cheeks flush as he realized he'd been staring.

"So you just here slumming or what?" Jaybird asked.

"Or did Mr. Big Shot Datajacker get homesick?" Snatcher added.

"Biz," Tommy said. "Here on biz."

"Biz that'll get us thrown in jail again?" Z Dog said. Tommy wasn't sure if Z was joking or not.

"Hey," he shot back, "we got you out, didn't we? Got the charges dropped too."

Z Dog grinned, but there was no humor in it. "Dangerous company you are, Tommy fucking Thai."

Tommy stepped forward. "Playing in the big leagues make you nervous, bruh? Stealing handbags from old ladies more your speed?"

Girlie, Snatcher, and Jaybird erupted in laughter. Z Dog stared blankly at Tommy, then after a few moments his face broke into a grin, this one genuine. He shoved Tommy playfully and said, "Salty fuck. You were always a salty fuckity fuck."

"So give it up, TT. What kind of biz?" Girlie asked.

"I'm looking for somebody," Tommy said. "She's a turfie, but older than us. Goes by Blayze. Any of you seen her around here lately?"

All four Anarchy Boyz looked at each other knowingly.

Z Dog lifted his chin at Tommy. "Funny you should ask, bruh."

* * *

Hiding out in a hiverise had pros and cons. On the upside, the vast complexes always had plenty of long-forgotten spaces no one used. Abandoned workshops or offices or even entire floors. Every hiverise brat who'd ever played hide-and-seek could tell you there was no shortage of places you could disappear into. The downside was those places were usually abandoned for a reason. Too many rats. No power connections. A dangerously sagging floor. The deserted nooks and crannies of a hiverise were often so forbidding, even squatters avoided them.

But the biggest downside was you had to get to your hiding spot in the first place, which meant you were going to be seen by someone. Usually a lot of someones. And in the cramped, crowded environs of a hiverise, gossip traveled fast. Tommy hadn't been sure Blayze would come to New Fulton to hide out. That much had been a guess, and he'd told Maddox as much. Under pressure, people often fled to places they knew, places where they felt safe. Bail jumpers were almost always recaptured at obvious sanctuaries like their girlfriend's or mom's home. And while Blayze was far smarter than some bail-jumping thug, you never knew what someone might do in a panic.

He figured he had a one-in-ten chance of finding her here. And if she had run for shelter at NF, his turfies would likely know about it.

She had and they did, as it turned out.

"Let me guess," Tommy said. "She's in that new tower on the west end?"

"You got it," Z Dog said, adding that he'd seen Blayze and a small entourage arrive the previous morning. "She had it put up a few months ago. Guess she's rolling in the cash these days. Not that I give a shit."

"Not that anybody gives a shit," Girlie added. "Not about that bitch."

"What, you got bad blood with her or something?" Tommy asked.

"Who *doesn't* have bad blood with her?" Z answered. "Whenever she's around, this whole place gets turned upside down. She has her thugs shake down every stand in the food court. Never pays for a single meal. Then she has them shut down every hallway anywhere near her precious little tower, tossing people out of their digs like they were stray dogs or squatters or something. Whole families, bruh, kicked out of their digs just because they live nearby. That's not right." He shook his head in disgust, then spat on the ground. "Every time she comes around, it's like some fucking plague hits this place. They even broke Jaybird's hand, saying he was revving his motor too loud. Can you believe that shit?"

Tommy looked over at Jaybird, who raised up his hand and nodded. He had a big wrap around his wrist and a couple of his fingers bent at unnatural angles. "Crushed it in a shop vise, bruh," Jaybird said. "I can still use it, but it don't work like before."

Tommy turned back to Z. "Can you get me to that tower?"

"Of course I can," Z said without hesitation. "You think I can't find my way around their lame-ass blocked hallways? But why would you want to go there?"

"Biz," Tommy said. "Heavy biz."

"You sure, bruh?" Z Dog asked.

"Yeah."

Z shrugged. "All right, Tommy Thai. If that's where you got to be, I can get you there. But don't say I didn't warn you."

Leaving his ride with his turfies, Z led Tommy inside the hiverise. The pair made their way down a dimly lit windowless corridor. Tommy hadn't been down this winding hallway in years, but the path came back to him quickly. He knew every corner of NF's insides, every dead-end path, every corrugated aluminum sheet of its ramshackle roof. Even with the time away, the map in his head hadn't faded at all.

"Who's the best climber on the crew?" Tommy asked.

"You are," Z answered.

"Besides me."

Z Dog thought about it. "Girlie, I suppose, why?"

Tommy told him why, asking for a favor.

"Sure," Z said, nodding. "I think she can do that for you." He donned his specs, a cheap pair of knockoff Venturellis. "Let me call her."

* * *

"Here we go," Z Dog said minutes later, keeping his voice low. "Two more lefts and we're there. They've been hiding out up there since they showed up yesterday. Got a couple hard types watching the door."

"Thanks, Z," Tommy said. "I got it from here."

"What?"

"I said I got it from here." Z started to protest, but Tommy cut him off. "This is really hot water, bruh."

Z shrugged. "So what's a little hot water to an Anarchy Boy?"

"I mean it," Tommy insisted. He hadn't forgotten how his friends had suffered on his account. Months ago when the police had a manhunt operation hunting Maddox, they'd picked up the Anarchy Boyz, interrogated them with fists and shocksticks, then thrown them in jail. His turfies hadn't cracked under the beatings and threats, hadn't given the cops a single word that might help them find Tommy and his datajacker boss.

"I don't want the A Boyz mixed up in this, Z," he said.

Z Dog laughed, shaking his head. "You don't get it. The Anarchy Boyz are *already* mixed up in this." He punched Tommy lightly on the shoulder. "If you're in it, we're in it, bruh. Simple as that."

Tommy stood there without speaking, overcome with emotion.

"Jesus," Z said, "you're not going to kiss me or something, are you?"

The tension broken, Tommy made an up-and-down motion with his fist. "Quick hand job, maybe?"

Z pushed him playfully. "Get out, you perv." He then turned his attention down the corridor. "All right, now," he whispered, stepping forward. "Just follow my lead, okay?"

At the next corner, Z Dog paused, holding his hand up for Tommy to stop, and cautiously peered around the wall. He then padded over to Tommy and whispered, "You stay right here, bruh."

Tommy did as he was told, knowing anything could happen in the next few moments. Z Dog was a brilliant street con, but he was as unpredictable as he was clever. Tommy had seen him pull off some incredible scams, but he'd also seen more than a few incredible fails, ending with Z getting punched out or arrested.

Z gave Tommy a wink and began whistling casually as he ambled around the corner with a notable spring in his step. Tommy held his breath and listened.

"Gentlemen," Z Dog said with all the sincerity of a street vendor greeting a clueless tourist. "Can I interest you in some of New Fulton's finest locally sourced pharmaceuticals?"

"Get lost, kid," a voice said. "We look like pharma freaks to you?"

"I'll give you the new customer discount," Z said. "Half price for a six-pack of deliriums. Send you straight to Mars and keep your prick hard for three hours straight, no lie."

"Fuck off," a second voice said.

"Come on, guys," Z pleaded. "Half price. You can't beat that anywhere in the City."

Tommy peeked around the corner. Twenty meters away, Z stood in front of the two guards. He looked tiny, like a monkey standing in front of two gorillas. And both gorillas had pistols in hip holsters. To Tommy's relief, they hadn't drawn them yet.

"Kid, I'm telling you, get the fu—"

"Come on, guys," Z cried out, "don't tell me your ladies wouldn't like a nice hard HARD

PREEEECK!"

On the last word, to both the guards' and Tommy's utter shock, Z grabbed both men by the crotch and squeezed. The guards gasped and flailed, taken completely by surprise, and floundered backward. In the next moment, Z released them and tore down the corridor, disappearing around a corner and screaming, "HARD PREEEECK, HARD PREEEECK!"

"You little fuck!" one guard shouted, and then both ran after him, fumbling for their guns and leaving the stairwell to the tower unguarded.

Z fucking Dog, Tommy thought. What a piece of work. It hadn't been the most sophisticated distraction, but hell if it hadn't worked like a charm. Tommy rushed to the stairs and began the long climb up.

From the outside, the new tower had appeared to reach about fifteen stories high. The structure was narrow, making the stairs steep by architectural necessity, and every four meters or so there was a landing. No two landings were alike in material. Plank wood one level. Brushed aluminum the next. Like much of the rest of NF's expansions, the tower and its internal stairway appeared cobbled together and, to the naked eye, structurally unsound. But somehow everything held together, even solidly so. Tommy climbed up another set of stairs.

He put on his specs, blinked up the mic's sensitivity to max. Pausing for a moment, he listened as he watched the audio monitor superimposed on the lens. No sounds of footsteps on the stairs. No one coming after him. Z was probably still running them in circles, the nutjob.

Finally, he reached the top, catching his breath on a wide landing of grated steel. Daylight poked through gaps in the patchwork walls of corrugated aluminum and fiberboard. At the far end of the landing stood a door.

Tommy removed his specs and hung them on his shirt collar. Taking a deep breath to gather himself, he stepped forward and knocked on the door. After what felt like a very long wait, a voice from behind the door snapped, "Who the fuck are you?"

Tommy stared into the round glass of the old-fashioned peephole. "Tell Dezmund and Blayze Tommy Park is here."

A short silence followed by an unintelligible exchange in hushed voices.

"How'd you get past security?" the voice demanded.

"What security?" Tommy said. "I didn't see any security. Just came right up the stairs."

"Get your hands where I can see them."

Tommy obliged, showing his hands. A moment later the door opened and a burly man with a shaved head popped out onto the landing. He began frisking Tommy, running his big hands roughly over arms and legs. When he finished, the bald man hustled Tommy through the doorway. "He's clean," the man called out.

Inside was a narrow-walled anteroom with a high ceiling and a single pendant light hanging a meter over Tommy's head. The man shoved Tommy into the next room. The small sitting area wasn't as nice as Beatrice's hotel suite, but it was close. Plush furniture, granite tile floors, and the walls looked like a regular building's walls, smooth and white. The sudden contrast to the poor, shanty-like conditions found throughout New Fulton threw him for a moment, until he noticed Dezmund and Blayze standing at the far end of the room.

Blayze approached him, removed the specs from his shirt collar, and tossed them to Dezmund. She waved the bald man away, and he left the three of them alone.

"Who told you we were here?" Dezmund asked.

"Nobody," Tommy said. "I just had a hunch."

"Where's Maddox?" Blayze demanded.

"I don't know. We got separated."

The girl's eyes narrowed. "Separated how?"

"Just separated, you know." Tommy shrugged. "He ran down one street, I ran down another."

"Have you talked to him?" she asked.

"No, I haven't." From their skeptical looks, it was clear they weren't buying his story. "I swear, I haven't," he insisted.

Blayze and Dezmund exchanged a look. "Why are you here, kid?" Dezmund asked.

Tommy took a breath. "Listen, I know you tried to take him out, and I know why you did it. I came here to tell you I didn't have anything to do with those deals he stole. I even told him not to do it, but you think he listened to me?"

"Kid," Dezmund said, "do you think we're stu—"

Blayze gripped his arm, cutting him off. "Hang on a second, Dez." She stepped forward, looking Tommy up and down in a way that somehow managed to both unnerve and excite him.

Her face close to his, he felt her breath warm on his cheek. It was dizzying, intoxicating.

"If we did try to take him out," she said, "and I'm

not saying we did, wouldn't this be the last place in the world you'd want to be? Wouldn't we be the last two people you'd want to be standing in front of, unarmed and helpless?"

Tommy swallowed. "I'm here on biz, Blayze."

Blayze lifted her eyebrows. "Are you now? And what kind of business would that be?"

"Remember when you asked me if I was interested in moving up? I told you I'd let you know if anything changed."

"I remember."

"Well," Tommy said, shrugging, "I guess things have changed."

15
PUSHING TOMMY

"It's bullshit," Dezmund said. "Maddox has to be setting a trap for us."

Blayze sat across from Dez in the small room. The kid was outside, handcuffed to the landing, watched by their body man, Kres. Unlike the two meatheaded locals they'd hired to watch the ground-level entryway, Kres was an actual professional.

Like Dez, Blayze hadn't bought the kid's story about how he wanted to change teams, how he'd had enough of being on a two-man crew. The kid was a good liar, though. She had to give him that. The performance he'd given had been a convincing one. Inwardly, she wondered if that was because there was an element of truth in it. If there was some part of the kid that really wanted to come over. Maybe the whole charade hadn't entirely been an act.

"I say we let Kres have a little chat with him," Dez suggested.

Kres could certainly beat it out of the kid. Their body man was a particularly gifted interrogator. That was the easiest play, and maybe the best one, given the circumstances. But if they went that way, it meant giving up her own sway over the kid. Tommy obviously had a thing for her. She'd seen it right away, from the first moment they'd locked stares at Maddox's bar. It was like that sometimes. A kind of sixth sense she had. She knew at a glance, with absolute certainty, that she had power over someone, that she could bend them to her will. It had been the same way with Dez. If they unleashed Kres on the kid, the spell she had Tommy under would break. He'd hate her, fear her, resent her.

"I don't know if that's the way to go," she said.

Dez furrowed his brow. "Look, if Blackburn's lackey knows we're here, then he knows we're here too. That gives him the upper hand. We can't just sit here and wait for him to make a move. We have to squeeze the kid, get him to spill what his boss is up to."

"I know, I know," she conceded, blowing out a frustrated breath.

"I told you we shouldn't have come here," Dezmund said.

Blayze looked at him crossly but said nothing. Because for once the little bitch was right. It had been a dumb idea to hide out here, if she was being honest with herself. A rash decision she now wished he would have talked her out of. But she couldn't change it now, and there was no point in looking backward.

She tried to step outside of herself, tried to see things from the old jacker's point of view. Why would he send the kid here? Unarmed and pretending he wanted to change teams? What leverage did that get him? Why would he think they'd buy it?

"Maybe it's not a trap at all," she speculated.

"Maybe he's just buying himself time. He knows sending the kid here would throw us off-balance. So maybe he doesn't care if we can see through it, as long as it gives him enough time to get himself out of the City."

Dezmund looked skeptical. "Throwing the kid under the bus? I don't know."

"Why not? He did the same thing in his bar the other night without a second thought."

"Yeah, but that was just a game."

Again, the little bitch had a point.

Was the kid a distraction? Some kind of fake-out?

Maddox might have been past his datajacking prime, but there was no doubting he was still clever, and deviously so. The kind who laid traps within traps. The more she turned things over, the less certain she was about anything.

"I've got to call this in," she said, finally coming around to the topic they'd both been avoiding.

"No," Dezmund said abruptly. "Don't do that. We can handle this on our own. Let Kres go to work on the kid. He can get us what we need in five minutes."

"He told me," she reminded him. "Told us both, if you remember. If anything else went sideways, we had to reach out to him before we made any decisions." She shrugged helplessly. "I have to tell him, Dez."

As if on cue, her specs lying on the sofa arm began to blink. A call coming in. The pair exchanged a look, then Blayze picked up the lenses, put them on, and took a deep breath.

She opened the connection and said, "I was just going to call you."

* * *

The call had gone well. Better than expected, in

fact.

Dezmund had hoped they'd get instructions lined up with his way of thinking: letting Kres beat the crap out of the kid, in other words. Thankfully, Blayze had been given the green light to go the direction she preferred instead. So it would be no iron fist for Tommy Park. Well, not the Kres kind of iron fist, anyway. And if she failed, they'd have to use Kres as Plan B.

But she wasn't going to fail.

Alone with Tommy in her private suite, Blayze sat in a soft leather chair, staring at the kid. He stood two meters in front of her, with his arms held tight at his sides by wrist clamps embedded in the wall. Two more clamps bound his ankles, holding his feet shoulder-length apart. He was still fully clothed, for now.

"I like you, Tommy," Blayze said, crossing her legs. "Do you know that?"

The kid was nervous. They were always nervous the first time she restrained them. Her little bitches. How many had she had over the years? Dez was the latest, but before him it had been Isabel, then before Isa was Josh. She smiled inwardly at the memory of Josh, who always came in two minutes. He'd been so easy to break. And before Josh it had been Milody. And so now it was Tommy Park's turn. Her newest little bitch. Few things excited her more than breaking in a new one.

"What are you going to do to me?" the kid asked.

She ignored the question. "Of course you know I like you. You feel it, don't you? The same way I feel it from you. A kind of heat between us, a connection."

Rising from the chair, she opened a black case on

top of a table. Removing a shock wand from it, she took a step toward Tommy. When she activated the device, the kid flinched, his wide eyes fixed on the glowing tip.

"If you like me so much," he said, his voice cracking, "you sure got a weird way of showing it."

Blayze couldn't help but chuckle. In truth, she did like Tommy. And that would make this all the more fun.

"Mine's not what you'd call a conventional kind of affection," she said. With the wand's safety still on, she ran the hot end slowly down the front of Tommy's shirt, stopping at his crotch for a long moment. The kid's breath came in small little gasps, like he expected a shock to come any second. It was hot. So fucking hot. The tingling, the wetness between her legs was delicious.

Blayze took in a deep, cleansing breath. She couldn't let herself get carried away. Couldn't lose herself so much in the moment that she forgot the endgame, the whole reason she was doing this. She backed away from him, collecting herself.

"I know he sent you here," she said. "And I know all this business about switching crews is a cover story. Don't bother denying it."

"I told you, I haven't seen him or talked—"

She strode forward, tagging him on the belly with the wand. A loud snap and a sparking burst came from the wand's tip. The kid yelped and squirmed.

"Didn't I say don't bother denying it?" she scolded.

"Jesus!" the kid cried. "That hurt!"

She tossed the wand onto the chair. From the same black case she removed a pair of dressmaker's shears.

"What are those for?" the kid blurted.

"This doesn't have to hurt, you know," she said, turning again toward him.

"What are you going—"

"Can I tell you something, Tommy? Can I make a confession?" She took a step closer, holding the shears at her side. "I call a lot of the shots on Dez's crew. Who he hires, who he fires. Lots of other things too."

The kid's eyes didn't move from the blades in her hand.

"Tommy," she said softly, moving closer still. "Let's forget why you came here, all right? Let's just drop all that. Let's talk about the future. Your future." She smiled. "Our future."

She lifted the shears. The kid trembled visibly. Her face was nearly touching his. He squeezed his eyes shut and turned his head to one side. It took a tremendous act of self-control to keep her from thrusting her hand down the front of her pants. The little bitch thought she was going to cut him, slice him up.

Snip. His eyes still closed, Tommy recoiled at the sound and let out a small whimper.

Snip, snip. He was still stiff as a board, but now he seemed to be figuring it out. She wasn't cutting him.

She was cutting his clothes off.

He opened his eyes, looked down at the shirt being cut off of his torso with the precision of an emergency room technician. Piece by piece it fell to the floor. As did his pants a few moments later. He watched as she took his clothes away, saying nothing. The little bitch couldn't believe what was happening.

Blayze's underwear was a soaking mess.

She removed his shoes and socks last, leaving him naked. His body was pale and skinny and not much to look at, but he'd been blessed with a disproportionately large, perfectly symmetrical cock. She dropped the shears. They landed with a dull thud against the hardwood floor.

"Look at me," she said. He lifted his gaze from the floor to meet her eyes. "I think we could be friends," she said, unbuttoning her shirt. "Really good friends."

She undressed slowly. He watched her with an expression that was fearful and nervous, yet somehow still teeming with carnal lust. The anticipation, the kid's confused mixture of desire and distress were like some narcotic. If she could only freeze this moment, this feeling.

She pressed her body against his and he let out a shuddering breath. Her nipples pressed into his chest, she squeezed his upper arms as she placed her mouth next to his ear and whispered.

"Some people need guidance, Tommy. And that's okay. There's nothing wrong with it. I want us to be friends. I want to help you. I want to be here for you."

"Blayze," he said. "I…uh…I feel weird about this…"

He was bending. She could feel it. He'd break soon. She could feel that too. Feel it coming the way you knew an orgasm you were working your way toward was going to be a big one.

"It's time for you to move up, Tommy," she said. "You've earned it. You deserve it."

She felt him getting aroused, felt him hardening against her belly. Reaching down, she took him into her hand. "Mmmm, that's it."

Lifting her leg, she positioned herself to take him inside her. He moaned as she slid down onto him.

"I'd never embarrass you in front of anyone," she said in his ear, squeezing his arms as she ground into him. "Not like he did the other night. I want you to be with me, be on my crew, Tommy. I was us to be together."

The kid grunted and thrust his hips into her. "I want that too, Blayze. I want to be with you."

She kissed him, pressing her lips against his and shoving her tongue into his mouth. Feeling him wilt beneath her. Feeling him break. It was far more satisfying than any session she'd ever had with Dezmund.

But she couldn't finish. Not yet. She still had work to do.

"There's just one thing I need you to help me with, Tommy. One small thing."

"Tell me," he panted. "Tell me."

She had him. Hook, line, and sinker, as the old expression went. He was utterly and totally under her spell. Finally, she let herself surrender to pleasure, nearly passing out from the shuddering climax that hit her in wave after luscious wave.

Whoever said you couldn't mix business and pleasure had been a fool.

16
TERRIBLE AT GOODBYES

Maddox and Beatrice sat in the Royal Belmond's seventieth-floor hover platform, waiting for the airport limo. Next to Beatrice stood her only piece of luggage, a silver hard-shelled case, its handle extended. A light midday rain pattered against the curved glass overhang above their heads. Rivulets streamed down the sides in long streaks.

Both had on their specs, and both were busy subvocalizing commands. As Beatrice reviewed her job's contract renewal, Maddox checked for messages from Tommy. Still no update. The kid had sent a couple messages, stills captured from his lenses that let Maddox know he'd arrived at New Fulton. But after that the kid had gone incommunicado, which was worrisome. A born chatterbox, it wasn't like Tommy to go dark. They'd agreed to hourly check-ins, and the kid was nothing if not punctual. But for whatever reason—and Maddox couldn't think of a single good one—Tommy hadn't sent anything for the last three hours. No pics, no messages, nothing. The geotag on the kid's specs showed he was inside the hiverise, the icon pulsing like a tiny beacon in the map overlaid onto Maddox's lenses. But it hadn't moved in hours, which meant either the kid hadn't moved, or his specs were lying around somewhere and not on his face.

"What are you looking at?" Beatrice asked. She'd taken her specs off and was staring at Maddox.

He blinked away the map. "Just checking messages."

"Anything from the kid?"

"No."

Beatrice looked out from the platform. The City's great canyons of steel and glass and concrete lay beyond. "You really think he's all right? Or was that a line so I wouldn't worry?"

"He's fine," Maddox said. "He's not the reckless kid you remember."

For a long moment neither spoke. Beyond the platform's transparent enclosure, a thin trickle of luxury vehicles moved along the transit lanes, shuttling the highfloor wealthy back and forth, up and down. There were no advertisements this high up, no distractions to divert Maddox's attention from the awkwardness between him and the woman sitting next to him. In a way it reminded him of how he'd felt when he'd visited his ex, Lora, seeing her for the first time after many months apart. The helpless sense of knowing you should say something, but unable to get any words out or even know exactly what words were the right ones. The meat had limitations, as he often noted, and they weren't always physical.

"So what are you going to do?" she asked.

"Haven't really decided yet," he said. Another lie. How many would have to tell her before she left?

"This showdown stuff between you and this Dezmund is bullshit, you know," she said.

"It is what it is."

"And that's bullshit too."

"Look, I didn't start all this, but if I don't hit back and end it, I'm done. He'll keep coming after me."

Beatrice sighed in resignation, turning her head away from him. "Good afternoon, Ms. Washington," the vestibule said, using Beatrice's alias, "your shuttle will arrive in less than two minutes."

"You know what I hope, salaryman?" she asked, still looking away.

"What's that?"

She didn't answer right away. Standing up, she folded her arms and gazed out at the transit lane. "These mods I have don't last forever. The ones that make me strong and fast and help me think quicker. You have to refresh them after a while, upgrade to the latest and greatest if you want to keep up with the competition. At some point, though, your body says it's had enough. That's the stuff they put in the fine print when you sign off for a procedure, the stuff they always leave out of the marketing. Very few mods are permanent. And for hired muscle like me, when your body doesn't respond to mods the way it used to, or it even rejects them entirely, that's when you know it's time to get out of the business. But not everyone gets the message. When you've been kicking ass for twenty, thirty years, it's a hard thing to accept that you can't do it any longer. Your mind plays tricks on you, fools you into thinking you still have it. Like those sad boxers you see sometimes, years past their prime, convinced they can still get a title shot, refusing to accept they've lost a step or two. They have to get knocked out a few times before they finally figure it out. A lot of them never figure it out."

She took a long breath, let it out slowly. "I hope I'm not like that, salaryman. When it's time for me to get out of this business, I hope I can see it clearly."

"So it's my time to get out?" he asked. "That's what you think?"

She turned and looked at him. "It only matters what you think. I might have an opinion, but giving it to you wouldn't make a bit of difference. I know you better than that."

The limo shuttle arrived, hovering next to the platform, then sliding over and connecting with a soft hiss-clank.

"I don't think you're a has-been, salaryman," she said, "for the record. But in our world, not very many get to choose when they get out or how it happens. Maybe this is your chance to do that."

"Maybe it is," he found himself saying.

She reached for her luggage. "I've got a plane to catch. Take care of yourself, salaryman."

"You too."

There was no kiss, no embrace, only a look into one another's eyes and a shared nod. Maddox wasn't good at goodbyes. Neither of them was, it seemed.

Moments later she was gone, carried away by the limo. He stood on the platform watching the hover grow smaller, replaying her words in his head. He didn't entirely disagree with what she'd said. At some point he'd have to get out, and the longer he waited to do it, the more he tempted fate. But not today, and not on someone else's terms. Not if he could help it. And skipping the country to become a jobless houseboy in Canada wasn't exactly going out on a high note.

She could have helped you, boyo.

Maybe.

Maybe nothing. She would have and you know it.

Maybe I didn't want her help.

An incoming call chime interrupted the conversation in his head. Unknown caller, the feed said. Normally, he wouldn't have answered, but it could have been Tommy calling from a different pair of specs.

He answered, but it wasn't Tommy. It was an audio recording. And it was long. A quick scan told him it was a few hours in total. What in the world was this? Who had sent it? He fast-forwarded until he heard a voice he recognized.

"Holy shit," he said under his breath. For the next few minutes he listened raptly, amazed at the recording's contents. Then Tommy's skull and crossbones icon blinked on his lens.

"Kid," Maddox said, answering the call, "where the hell have you been?"

17
WASHINGTON SQUARE PARLEY

There were public places, and then there were public places. Washington Square Park was about as public as you could get. Covering ten acres in Lower Manhattan, the park, its central fountain, and its iconic marble arch at the northern entrance were instantly recognizable to first-time visitors to the City. The square had been featured in countless programs on the entertainment feeds. A green oasis of towering oaks and maples and thick shrubs, the park was one of the few spots in the City left unchanged by the passage of time. Some claimed it was one of the last remaining landmarks city bureaucrats still took civic pride in, unwilling to sell off any portion of it to real estate investors as they had with Central Park to the north, which had been reduced to half its original size, block by block, over the last century by public officials desperate to balance budgets or (more often) line their own pockets. Others said private benefactors maintained the square out of familial nostalgia, wealthy clans with long histories in the City whose forebears remembered a time before hiverises and megacities and hover traffic.

A fidgeting bundle of nerves, Tommy sat at the park's western edge in the shade of a sycamore's broad canopy. This section of the park was known as Chess Plaza, where matches were played on small tables with embedded chessboards. During the busy late-morning and afternoon hours, regulars occupied most of the tables, hustling tourists out of money with quick matches. Most ended in minutes, the locals besting even the most seasoned visiting players with bold, unconventional tactics. City chess was like the City itself. It was no place for the timid or the meek. It was aggressive, relentless, and it had no mercy for the innocent or the unprepared.

Four chairs surrounded the table, one of which was occupied by Tommy, two others by Dezmund and Blayze. The chair beside Tommy was empty as the trio waited for Maddox.

"He should have been here by now," Blayze said, checking the time on her specs.

"He'll be here," Tommy assured her.

Maddox was already five minutes late, which worried Tommy. His mentor was notoriously punctual, usually arriving minutes early to appointments and meetings. Traffic, Tommy told himself. Maybe he'd been caught in traffic. He wouldn't have bailed. Would he?

"There's our man," Dezmund said.

Tommy looked over. Maddox crossed the street at the corner of West Fourth and MacDougal, heading toward them. He blew out a breath of relief, though the knot in his stomach refused to untie itself. There was still a lot to be worried about. So many things could go wrong in the next few minutes.

With a nod to Tommy, Maddox sat, removed his specs, and laid them on the checkered tabletop. Tommy did the same, as did Dezmund and Blayze. The parley would be nakedfaced and unarchived, as agreed.

"You wanted to talk," Maddox said, "so talk."

"Good to see you too, old friend," Dezmund said.

Blayze said nothing, staring at Maddox.

Tommy's boss lit a cigarette, blew smoke, and returned the lighter to his pocket.

"We want a truce," Dezmund said.

"A truce?" Maddox echoed.

"That's right," Dezmund said.

"A little late for that, don't you think?" Maddox said. He nodded toward Blayze. "Why is she here? You taking her for ice cream after?"

"Screw you, jacker," she growled.

"You know, Dez, I've got the strangest feeling you don't have complete control of your shop." Maddox lifted an eyebrow. "Should I be dealing with you or is little girlie here in the driver's seat now?"

Damn, Tommy reflected. Maddox was sharp. And he was right on the money. The uncomfortable glance between Blayze and Dezmund all but confirmed the accusation.

Not that Tommy needed any confirmation, of course. Blayze had already proved to him, in a most convincing way, who was really running the show.

In hindsight, though, Tommy had had his suspicions during the training sessions for the BNO gig. He'd noticed how Dez treated Blayze differently than the others. To everyone else on the crew, he gave orders. To her, he offered suggestions. With others he was curt and blunt. With her he was polite, even respectful. And when she'd first approached Tommy about changing teams, there'd been something in her tone when she talked about the crew. It was like they worked for her, not for him.

Maddox drew on his cigarette. "All right," he said. "I might be down for a truce. But only on one condition."

"And what's that?" Dezmund asked.

"You tell me what this is really all about."

"You know what it's about."

"Come on, Dez," Maddox scoffed, blowing smoke. "Trying to take me out over a few small deals? I'm not buying it. That's not your style." He nodded again at Blayze. "And I'm not buying that she talked you into it either." He shifted his gaze back to his old colleague. "So what is it, Dez? Tell me."

Dezmund and Blayze exchanged another uneasy look. Neither answered.

Maddox turned to Tommy. "Kid, did I ever tell you about how Dez and I used to play chess here?"

Tommy shook his head.

Tapping the inlaid chessboard, Maddox said, "Right here, every Friday at noon. Sometimes I'd get lucky and win, but most of the time he did. He was a good player. He'd think ahead ten, fifteen moves. He could beat most of the hustlers around here, too, which drove them crazy. And do you know how he did it?" He locked his gaze on Dezmund. "He did it by never taking risks unless he had to. He never brought his queen out early. Never gave up a single pawn unless it gave him something better in return. Every move, without exception, had a reason behind it. Every small tactic lined up with a bigger strategy. You could see it when the game was over, when he'd beaten you, how he'd played it. Solid, mistake-free moves."

Maddox blew smoke. "And he jacked data the same way he played chess. Smart and careful, nothing left to chance. That's how he's lasted so long in this business. That's how he built up the best crew in the City. Yeah, maybe he struts around like some movie star, like he doesn't have a care in the world. But when it comes to the job, there's never been anyone more sober and serious. So what I don't get is why this guy I've known half my life, who's anything but reckless, would go to so much trouble, put so much on the line over a few small-time deals."

To Dezmund he said, "So, back to the question. What's all this really about? And don't give me some nonsense about jacker cred and reputation. It's not like the street knew I was undercutting you. Nobody outside of the people sitting around this table knew I was poaching your bids." He dropped his cigarette and crushed it under his shoe. "Tell me, old friend. I really want to know. Because it's not like you to bring out your queen out to capture a little pawn."

For a long moment no one spoke. Tommy's insides jumped around like he'd eaten bad Thai. He thought he noted a change in Dezmund's expression. The kind of look you saw on a card player's face when they weren't so sure about the strength of their hand.

Maddox seemed to notice it too. Or maybe he detected something more, something Tommy hadn't picked up on. In any case, Maddox apparently he didn't like what he saw, because he stood up suddenly and said, "Kid, let's get out of here."

Tommy remained seated.

"Kid," Maddox repeated.

Tommy averted his eyes from Maddox. He stared at the tabletop and said nothing.

"He's not going with you," Blayze said, smirking. "He's no fool, old man. He wants to move up in the world."

"He does, does he?" If Maddox shot his apprentice an angry or disappointed look, Tommy didn't see it with his eyes still cast downward. But from the top of his vision he glimpsed Maddox snapping his fingers at Dezmund. "Now *that's* the kind of thing you might start a war over, Dez," Maddox said. "Stealing someone else's crew. That shit's not cool."

Dezmund began to say something back, but his eyes moved beyond Maddox as something in the near distance drew his attention. Maddox turned to look, seeing what Tommy now noticed also: two large men in black suits, most of their faces obscured by oversized darkened specs, heading straight for them. Tommy scanned the area, finding two more similarly dressed thugs striding toward them from the opposite direction.

Maddox glared at Blayze. "What the hell is this?"

"Don't make a scene," she said calmly, "and they won't hurt you."

Tommy steeled himself for what was about to happen. Then he spotted a familiar face in the crowd, heading toward them. His mouth dropped open in shock.

What the hell was Beatrice doing here?

18
FOOLISH, FOOLISH WOMAN

Datajackers were good at a lot of things, Beatrice reflected. They could sneak into a secured datasphere like a digital ghost, unseen and undetected, steal a company's invaluable intellectual property, collect their fee from a grateful competitor, and deposit the proceeds in an orbital tax haven. All this they could pull off inside a minute or two. They were also experts at disappearing. The best datajackers knew how to erase their personal digital histories, birth records, even their criminal pasts, though this last was often difficult as law enforcement—when it came to datajacking crimes—had reverted to the ancient practice of keeping records on paper and microfiche to avoid such disasters. Still, datajackers were adept at the manipulation, deletion, and deception of all things digital. But they were far from perfect criminals. In Beatrice's experience, it was rare for a datajacker to have much in the way of criminal capabilities beyond their area of expertise. Sure, plug them into VS and they could work magic. But in the world of physical crime, most jackers were fish out of water, techie nerds who knew little about smuggling goods or running an underground gambling room or pimping out sex workers. They didn't know much about countersurveillance either. Case in point: the four datajackers sitting two tables away from her. Not a single one of them had the slightest clue she was watching them.

Beatrice sat facing an old dark-skinned man with a gray beard, her head down but eyes locked on the four datajackers. Minutes earlier, wearing a jacket with a large hood that covered her face in shadow, she'd planted herself in the empty chair across from the old man, who had a tented paper sign reading *10-minute game $200* handwritten in a dozen languages. His calling card for tourists who might want to challenge a local at the famous chess tables in Washington Square. Under her breath she offered triple his normal rate if he played slow while she kept an eye on her employer. The old man, taking her for a bodyguard, shrugged and said no problem, then moved his king's pawn forward two spaces.

"Your move," the man said. She pretended to stare at the board for a long moment, then advanced a knight.

Over at the other table, Maddox sat next to the kid. The salaryman was a pretty decent liar. As a professional thief, he had to be. The gift of deception was as fundamental to a datajacker's tool set as their specialized hardware and black market apps. They lied to intelligent systems and cybersecurity measures, masking their identities and fooling their way past the digital guardians of virtual space. They lied to cops about where they'd been and what they'd been doing on the night of the big data heist. Datajackers were born BS spinners, and you could save a lot of time and trouble by assuming everything that came out of their mouths wasn't true, believing only what their actions told you, not the actual words they said.

She'd thought Maddox was different in that respect, or at least different when it came to her. How utterly wrong she'd been. Until this morning he'd never lied to her, and she'd assumed that meant something. Foolish, foolish woman.

He'd lied to her about Tommy without so much as a blink, pretending not to know where the kid was, saying as much right to her face. She might not have caught it, but her gut told her something was wrong, and as he spoke she called up her thermal vision, a recent upgrade she'd acquired for her eye implants. The heat-sensitive view revealed a telltale flush of heat in the salaryman's cheeks. It was nothing more than a small surge of blood to the face, a tiny, involuntary bio-reaction. But it had been a reliably damning one. Maddox had lied to her.

So in turn she'd deceived him, ditching her ride to the airport once she was out of sight and tailing him the rest of the day. An impetuous reaction, for sure, especially for someone in her profession. The cold, steely part of her who cared about nothing but the job still nagged at her, telling her she should have written off the lying bastard and taken her scheduled flight out of town. But another part of her was too pissed off to listen, too stubbornly set on finding out why he'd deceived her.

And then there was Tommy. She couldn't leave without knowing whether the kid was in real trouble and, if it turned out he was, doing what she could to get him out of it. Maybe the salaryman didn't know the meaning of trust and loyalty, but she sure as hell did.

"It's your move," her opponent said, in a way that made her think he'd said it more than once. She looked down and nudged a pawn forward.

With the ambient noise of a crowded tourist spot and the jacket hood draped over her head, she couldn't make out what Maddox and company were discussing, even with her modded hearing. But then she didn't really have to. The scene unfolding a few feet away from her appeared to be a setup. There were four thugs dressed in black who kept looking over at them, doing a generally poor job of trying to stay inconspicuous as they wandered about the area. Not exactly your top-notch professionals, the four of them. Probably nightclub bouncers working a side gig.

Still, even if they weren't hardened criminals, they outnumbered her four to one. She was armed, but so were they. Inside two of their sport coats she'd spotted shoulder holsters, and if two of them were packing, it was a safe bet all of them were. Disrupting their plans would be no easy task.

Dezmund and the girl Blayze wouldn't take out Maddox, not here. Not with dozens of street cams, a crowd of eyewitnesses, and the heavy police presence common to every tourist spot in the City. She'd already seen three rhino-armored patrol cops in the two minutes since she'd taken her seat. They'd have to get him out of here first, which meant at some point the four glorified bouncers would converge on him, show him their guns, and discreetly usher him into an alleyway or maybe a ground car.

As if on cue, an unmarked white van pulled up to a

nearby loading zone. The driver got out, opened the side door, then stood there with his arms folded across his chest as he scanned the crowd. His gaze fell first on Maddox's table, then to the nearest of the four thugs, to whom he gave an almost imperceptible nod.

Given the odds, a distraction was the best option, though she had difficulty coming up with a tactic. It had to be something restrained and low-key. Enough to throw the thugs off guard for a moment or two so she could hustle Maddox and Tommy safely away, but not so disruptive it attracted police scrutiny or set off a crowd panic.

While she tried to come up with options, no small part of her wanted to get up, walk away, and leave Maddox to his fate. The cold, battle-hardened part of her. Wash her hands of the whole dirty business and get out of this teeming cesspool of a city. It wasn't her fight, was it? If it weren't for the kid, she most likely would have bailed already.

"Your move," the old man said again. A few tables over Maddox started to rise up from his chair, as if he was leaving. She scanned the crowd, spotting two of the hired thugs, both heading straight for the salaryman.

She had to move quickly. Standing up, she slid her way through the crowd. Inside her jacket, she found the rubber grip of the hand-sized shockstick, a miniature version of the same weapon used by police, only with a much smaller charge only good for two or three uses. She headed straight for the table where the salaryman stood. His features knotted in worry as he spotted the thugs striding toward him. As she passed close enough to Maddox to reach out and touch him,

Beatrice tucked the shockstick beneath her free arm and jammed it into a tourist, a large man with a half-eaten hot dog in his hand. The man gasped at the poke and glanced down, then as Beatrice thumbed the switch, he cried out and collapsed to the ground in a twitching, convulsing heap.

"Heart attack!" someone shouted. A crowd of onlookers formed around the man, gazing down at him in open-mouthed stares.

"Is there a doctor? Is someone here a doctor?" a woman cried frantically.

Maddox and his three datajacker companions gawked at the man, distracted by the sudden outbreak of human drama. Even the thugs paused to look, caught off guard by the unexpected scene. In the confusion Beatrice grabbed Maddox and Tommy by the arm and pulled them away from the table.

Maddox's eyes grew wide. "What are you doing here?"

Tommy's face knotted in confusion. "B? Thought you left town, mama."

"Let's get out of here," Beatrice said. "Keep your heads down."

Maddox yanked his arm away. "What do you think you're doing?"

"Saving your ass, as usual," she answered. "Though God knows why."

"You're screwing everything up," he said.

"Listen," she hissed. "Your friends want to throw you into that van over there, put a bullet in you, and dump you in the Hudson. Come on, let's go, now."

"B," Tommy said, "you really should have—"

"Don't move," a gruff voice behind her said. In the same moment she felt pressure against her lower back. One of the thugs pressing the muzzle of his gun into her.

The thug's three associates were suddenly there, surrounding her and Tommy and Maddox.

Beatrice swore inwardly. She'd almost gotten them out.

19
NO SELLOUT

"Poaching someone else's crew," Maddox said. "That shit's not cool."

Uncool but not unexpected, he added inwardly. In fact, he would have been surprised if they hadn't tried. He wondered for a moment who'd come up with the idea of turning the kid but then quickly answered his own question. She had, of course. She was the brains behind the whole thing, behind Dezmund's entire operation. Dez had even hinted around it before, hadn't he? That night his crew had shown up in Maddox's bar, when he'd mentioned how he was looking forward to getting out of the game. If Maddox had been paying closer attention, maybe he would have come to the conclusion then.

Dezmund began to say something, then stopped, his gaze shifting to something in the crowd. Maddox looked and spotted two men in black suits with oversized specs concealing most of their faces. Striding shoulder to shoulder, they headed straight for him. Then he spotted two more, coming at him from the opposite direction.

He glared at Blayze. "What the hell is this?"

She gave him a wry smile. "Don't make a scene, and they won't hurt you."

The girl had balls, no doubt about it. Kidnapping him in broad daylight, in a crowded public space, was a bold move. It was also exactly the move he'd counted on.

As the suited thugs closed in, Maddox spied a white van parked in a nearby loading area. The driver opened its sliding door, then stood next to it with his arms folded, trying his best to look nonchalant.

"That my ride over there?" he asked Blayze.

"Our ride," she said. "I thought it would be better if we finished our chat in private."

A sudden commotion broke out nearby. Two meters away from their table, a large man lay on the ground, twitching and convulsing.

"Heart attack!" someone shouted, then another voice cried out for a doctor. A knot of onlookers quickly formed around the man, jostling Maddox as they drew near. He looked away from the spectacle, trying to find the thugs, but he'd lost them in the excited chaos the stricken man had caused.

In the next instant Beatrice was there, appearing as if out of thin air.

"What are you doing here?" he asked reflexively.

"B?" Tommy cried, standing up. "Thought you left town, mama."

"Let's get out of here," she said, already pulling him away.

He yanked his arm from her grip and tried to tell her she was screwing things up, but she wouldn't listen. A second later they were surrounded by the four thugs.

"Don't move," one of them grunted at Beatrice, sliding a pistol discreetly into her back.

Maddox felt a second pistol thrust into his own back. "Easy," the thug behind him said. "Nice and easy, jacker."

The men in suits ushered them away from the chaotic scene as Dezmund, Blayze, and Tommy followed close behind.

"Get them in the van," Blayze ordered. Over by the fallen man, a rhino-armored cop had arrived, and an ambulance siren wailed in the distance. The thugs maneuvered Maddox and Beatrice through the crowd toward the waiting van.

"Where's the driver?" Blayze asked one of the thugs. The man who'd been waiting by the van was no longer there.

The suited thug looked puzzled. "I don't—"

A screaming noise suddenly filled the square, hitting Maddox's eardrums so hard he flinched. Damn, those machines were loud.

The first Anarchy Boy burst into view a block away, his bike's engine screaming as he zoomed down the pedestrian walkway toward the square. Tourists and locals leapt out of his way as he tore down the avenue, barreling straight for Maddox and company. Another biker appeared in the opposite direction, coming at them just as fast.

The kids had timed it perfectly, Maddox noted.

"Tommy, get down!" Maddox shouted as he dropped to his knees. Tommy quickly followed suit, crouching down low to the pavement.

"What the—?" one of the thugs blurted as the first bike screamed past, his words cut off by a blow to the head. The rider whooped and hollered and waved a small pipe around as he tore down the walkway. The second rider attacked simultaneously with the first, spinning a chain over her head like some demon cowboy's steel lasso. She took out a second thug, shattering the man's specs and slashing his face as she whizzed past. The man spun around and fell, clutching his face and howling. The two uninjured thugs, stunned and confused by the sudden attack, forgot their captives and moved to help their associates.

Maddox sprang to his feet and made his move quickly, bear-hugging Dezmund from behind; Tommy did the same with Blayze. Clutching the two tightly, Maddox and Tommy dove into the van, crashing onto the hard floor in a heap of bodies. The van's tires squealed and smoked as the vehicle shot away. Fighting to keep his balance, Tommy reached over and slid the door shut with a loud metallic bang. The last image Maddox had of Washington Square before the door closed was Beatrice staring at him, her mouth gaping open in surprise, and the two uninjured thugs leaping up to their feet and running after them.

"They've got a car," Tommy said, breathing heavily. "They'll be coming after us."

"Get off of me!" Blayze cried. Confused, she raised herself to a crouching stance as the vehicle rocked and bumped along.

"You wanted to finish that chat in private, yeah?" Maddox said. He released Dezmund and stood, pressing his palm against the roof for balance. "Well, so do I."

"You fucking amateurs," she snapped. She lurched to the partition separating the cargo space from the cabin. Rapping her knuckles on the narrow connecting window, she cried out, "Coop, stop the van, now!"

The window slid open, and a kid with a green mohawk who definitely wasn't Coop shouted back, "Who the hell is Coop, baby?"

"That big fook you knocked on the head a minute ago, Z," Tommy answered.

"Oh, yeah," Z Dog said. "Coop was kind of a dick." He held up a pair of oversized lenses. "Nice specs, though." Then to Blayze: "Sorry, baby, I only take orders from my boys Blackburn and Tommy Thai."

Blayze kicked the partition in anger, then spun to the door and began yanking on the handle. It didn't move.

"It's locked from up here," Z Dog called back. "Safety first, baby. Just sit back and relax."

"Christ," Dezmund said, shaking his head in disbelief. With his back against the wall, he stomped his foot against the floor. "I knew it. I fucking knew it. I told you he was smart, didn't I? Now look at us."

"Shut up!" she shouted, furious. Then she whirled away from the partition to face Tommy. The kid stood next to Maddox, his hand also pressed against the roof.

Tommy grinned at Blayze. "Sorry to disappoint, mama," he said, "but I ain't no sellout."

"You filthy groundfloor piece of shit," she spat. "I should have cut off your prick when I had the chance."

Maddox turned to the kid. "The mouth on this one."

"I know, right?" Tommy said. "She's got anger

issues too."

"You really hit that?" Maddox asked.

"Seemed like a good idea at the time, bruh."

Blayze's face contorted with fury, her teeth bared like some rabid dog. Enraged beyond speech, she looked as if the top of her head might blow off.

From the driver's compartment, Z Dog shouted, "Ah, shit!"

"What?" Maddox called.

"We've got company," Z said. "Coming up on our ass."

Maddox grabbed a wall handhold as the van leaned into a corner, tires screeching. He turned and peered out the small rear window. The vehicle rocked back and forth violently as the kid weaved through traffic. Through the glass Maddox saw them, the two uninjured thugs in a black Lexus, pursuing them. He cursed inwardly. Car chases in the City's sluggish traffic always favored the hunter, never the hunted.

Later, Maddox would regret turning his back on Dezmund for that small moment. The punch came from Maddox's blind side, striking him flush on the temple. Outside the van's window the City lurched sideways. Maddox reeled, falling against the wall of the van. Before he could regain his balance, a follow-up kick to his gut knocked the wind from his lungs. He dropped to his knees, gasping for air. Dezmund loomed over him, fists clenched.

Then a gun fired. Inside the small enclosure of the van's cargo space, the shot's deafening report struck Maddox violently, as if someone had jabbed a needle into his eardrums. The ringing in his ears instantly drowned out all other sounds. With an effort, he sucked in a breath and saw Tommy standing near the cab, holding up a small homefabbed pistol Z Dog had passed back to him. Smoke drifted up from the weapon's thin barrel, and a ray of daylight shone down through a thumbnail-sized hole in the van's roof.

"Over in the corner," Tommy barked at Dezmund and Blayze, waving the gun.

Gasping and still woozy, Maddox got to his feet and moved over to Tommy as Dez and Blayze did as they were told. Z Dog passed back two pairs of plastic cuffs, and Maddox bound the datajackers' hands behind their backs. No easy task when you're dizzy with the floor rocking under your feet. He'd just finished binding their wrists when the van stopped abruptly, sending its passengers in the cargo space lurching forward.

"What's going on?" Maddox asked, bracing himself against the partition.

Z Dog twisted around to face Maddox. "I kind of turned into a dead-end alley, bruh. Sorry, yeah?"

"So back it up," Maddox said.

"Not sure I can do that right now," the kid said, lifting his hands slowly off the steering wheel and raising them over his head.

The two thugs stood near the front of the van with their pistols drawn.

"Get out," one of them barked, throwing open the driver's door.

Maddox locked eyes with Tommy. "Give it to me," he said quietly, holding out his hand.

Tommy hesitated. "I can take care of—"

"Tommy, give me the gun."

The kid blew out a breath, then nodded and passed Maddox the weapon.

"They're armed!" Blayze shouted, popping up to her feet. "They've got a fabbed pist—"

Her words were cut short by Tommy's fist striking her mouth. She fell backwards onto the floor. "You cheap little hood," she hissed, spitting blood. "I'm going to have your fucking head on a stick."

"Out, now!" the thug repeated, louder. "And hands where I can see them!"

Maddox took a breath. "Go ahead and get out," he advised Z Dog. "Don't give them a reason."

Out of the back window he saw the parked Lexus, blocking their way out of the alley. He looked down at the toylike cherry red weapon in his hand. A three-shotter, of course. And Tommy had already used one. He couldn't waste either of the remaining bullets with a missed shot.

He'd take out the nearest one first, the one on the driver's side. Maddox steeled himself, crouching low and creeping forward. Raising up slightly to peer through the cab window, Maddox saw Z Dog standing outside the van near the front bumper, his hands clasped behind his neck. The thugs were no longer in view. They must have backed away when they heard Blayze's warning.

Z Dog's eyes suddenly went wide, and his hands unclasped and dropped to his sides. Maddox thought for an instant the kid was about to be shot, then he heard a grunt and something slammed hard against the outside of the van.

"Nice moves!" Z Dog shouted. It was a joyful cry, Maddox realized, not a terrified one. What was happening out there?

In the next moment, on the opposite side of the impact, the second thug staggered into view.

Hunched forward, his eyes squeezed shut in agony, his forgotten pistol lay on the ground behind him. Riding on his back was Beatrice, her arms locked around his neck in a choke hold, her legs wrapped around his belly. The man lunged backward onto the ground, twisting and kicking and clawing at his neck. Useless efforts, as Beatrice had him locked in tight. Seconds later, the thug's body went limp. He was out cold.

Releasing him, Beatrice rose to her feet, brushed herself off, and reached inside the driver's area to unlock the cargo door. A moment later she slid the door open, and behind her the other thug lay sprawled out. Dead or unconscious, Maddox wasn't sure.

Beatrice held out her hand. "Give me that thing," she said to Maddox, "before you hurt somebody."

Maddox passed her the pistol, relieved to surrender the weapon. He wasn't good with guns.

Beatrice glanced between Maddox, Tommy, and their two cuffed prisoners. She tucked the fabbed pistol into her jacket pocket, then put her hands on her hips.

"You've got some explaining to do, salaryman."

20
NICE TRY, SALARYMAN

Since the thugs no longer needed it, Maddox and
company piled into the Lexus, the cuffed datajackers
wedged into the back between Tommy and Z Dog.
Maddox sat next to Beatrice, who drove until she
found a deserted parking garage a few blocks away.
Thankfully, Maddox reflected, there were no police
on their tail. The alley where she'd taken the thugs by
surprise hadn't had any working street cams, and
whatever portions of the chase—and calling the
minute-long sprint before they turned into a dead end
a chase was a stretch—had been detected apparently
hadn't kicked off any automated alarms. Traffic-
monitoring algorithms generally ignored speedy, even
foolhardy drivers if their recklessness didn't cause an
accident or last more than a few moments. Wrecks,
hit-and-runs, and other major crimes invariably got
flagged to the nearest patrol cop. Shitty drivers, not so
much.

Beatrice and Maddox got out and moved a discreet
distance away from the Lexus while the two kids kept
an eye on the sullen captives. She'd lent Tommy her

Ruger to make sure their guests stayed put.

"All right," she said, crossing her arms and scowling. "Spill it. And this time no bullshit." They stood in a darkened corner of the dilapidated concrete structure. From the construction site on the adjacent lot, the grinding motor of an excavator machine drowned out the City's normal symphony of ground car klaxons, advertisement jingles, and the crowd churn of countless pedestrians.

Might as well, Maddox decided, his temple still throbbing from Dezmund's sucker punch. There didn't seem to be much point in keeping anything from her at this point.

"The kid thought they might hide out in New Fulton," Maddox said, "and I figured it was worth checking out." While Beatrice had been out on her shopping run, he explained, he and Tommy had talked it over.

As she listened, her scowl deepened. "Christ, you used the kid as bait…*again*?"

"It wasn't like that."

"I'm sure it wasn't."

"Listen," he said, yearning for a smoke in the worst way, "he was only supposed to check things out. That's what we'd agreed to. See if they were there and then get back to me. But what can I say, the kid improvised. And not too badly, if you ask me."

Tommy had called Maddox, he explained, apparently as Blayze and Dezmund had requested. The pair had no doubt listened in on the call, connecting via their own specs and muting their mics. They weren't going to take any chances. They wouldn't let Maddox pull a fast one on them.

What they didn't know was that Tommy had

already pulled a fast one of his own.

By the time he'd arrived at Blayze and Dezmund's tower hideout, Tommy's turf sister Girlie had completed the favor Z Dog had asked for on Tommy's behalf. The skilled climber had scaled the outside of the new tower and stealthily implanted listening devices called "little ears" into the walls. After testing the link and making sure the little ears were picking up every word from inside the tower suite, she'd then set the autosend to the number Tommy had passed along: Maddox's private line. The recording had loaded onto Maddox's specs a few minutes prior to Tommy's call. And by the time the call had come in, Maddox had heard just enough to gather what the kid had done, and so he'd played along during their chat, agreeing to the meetup.

"After the call," he explained, "I went through the recording until I found what they were up to."

Everything was there. How they planned to kidnap him. Where they'd park the van. Which direction they'd converge on him in Washington Square Park. And once they had him in the van, it would be two shots to the head, then dump him in the Hudson. He'd learned every detail of their planned ambush and execution, thanks to Tommy's quick thinking.

The only portion of the recording he hadn't been able to decipher was a brief call Blayze had made. Or what he believed was a call. Either that or she'd been muttering to herself. Whatever the short conversation had entailed, he couldn't decipher any of it, even after running it through filters. The little ears had picked up nothing but an unintelligible murmur. So either Blayze had some kind of chatter bubble-type tech in her lenses that distorted her speech or she'd been standing in an acoustically dead zone where the hidden mics couldn't pick her up. Either way, the entire conversation had been lost on him.

Still, he'd gleaned everything he really needed from the recording. And once he'd learned the specifics of their plan to get rid of him, it didn't take long for Maddox to work out how to undermine things. He called up the Anarchy Boyz, and as it turned out they were more than happy to help. Fortunately for Maddox, the biker gang apparently despised Blayze as much as he did, though he hadn't had time to delve into the reasons behind it.

"So those kids saved your ass again," Beatrice said. "How many favors do you owe them now?"

"I did get them out of jail, if you recall," Maddox countered.

She gave him a sour look. "They were there because of you in the first place, salaryman."

"Details," he said, shrugging. "Okay," he confessed, "maybe I owe them one."

So now she knew the whole story. Not that it appeared to make any difference. She still glared at him, her eyes burning with a heat he could feel.

"It wasn't exactly the most elegant piece of work, was it?" she asked.

"I didn't have much time to plan."

"I could have done this a lot better, you know," she said.

"Probably."

"So why didn't you ask me, then? Why'd you lie to me about knowing where the kid was and what you two were up to?"

There were answers to those questions. He knew there had to be. But searching his mind, he found no explanations, no sensible way to explain what he'd done.

"If the kid went with you, they would have found him," he finally said. "Sooner or later, they would have tracked him down. I figured if I kept him close, I could keep him out of trouble."

She gave him a mirthless smile. "Nice try, salaryman. But that's not it. That's not it at all."

"It's not?"

"I thought you trusted me," she said.

"I do trust you."

"Just not enough, I guess," she said. The anger faded from her voice and features, replaced with a wistful, disappointed expression. The man standing in front of her wasn't who she thought he was. Maddox wanted to say something, but again no words came.

Maybe she was right. Maybe he didn't trust her, even though she'd given him every reason to. Her disappointment struck him powerfully, the way the truth sometimes does when you don't expect to hear it.

But it wasn't just about trust, he insisted inwardly. Yes, he'd lied to her. But he'd done it for reasons not just rooted in his own flaws and inadequacies. He'd lied to her because he wanted her out of it. He and Tommy had targets painted on their backs already, but she hadn't been implicated. And he wanted to keep it that way.

The world was an awful place, filled with awful people. He could count on one hand the number of people who'd ever given a damn about him, and he'd still have a couple fingers left over. Rooney, Tommy, and the disappointed mercenary woman standing in front of him now. That was it. Roon was gone, and

Tommy had been thrown to the wolves with him. So if he had to lie to Beatrice to keep her out of this dirty little war, then fine. He'd rather have her pissed off at him than dead.

She removed the fabbed pistol from her jacket and handed it to him. Then she tilted her head toward the Lexus. "Go and end your war, salaryman," she said. "I've got a plane to catch."

21
CONFESSION

Maddox watched as Beatrice walked away and reclaimed her Ruger from Tommy. She said something to the kid that Maddox couldn't make out, then touched him on the cheek and turned away, leaving the parking garage out a side door. A part of him wanted to follow after her and try to explain himself. But the larger part of him resisted, knowing whatever he might say wouldn't erase what he'd done and how she felt about it. He wished things could have been different, but there you were. Pissed off at him was better than dead, he reminded himself.

Blowing out a long breath, he steeled himself for the grim task at hand. He approached the Lexus, the pistol heavy in his hand.

"Get out," he said to Dezmund and Blayze. Their hands still bound behind them, the two datajackers scooted awkwardly across the back seat and exited the sedan.

Maddox waved the pistol. "Turn around and face the wall."

"You don't have to do this," Dezmund said, his

voice quaking. Even in the dim ambient light, Maddox could see the death panic on the man's face. He averted his eyes to Dezmund's midsection.

"I didn't start all this," Maddox said. "But I'm finishing it."

Anger welled up inside him. It never should have come to this. Why the hell hadn't Dezmund tried to work it out with him, before things had gone too far?

"I didn't start this either," Dezmund said.

Maddox glanced at Blayze. There was no fear on her face, only a cold, hateful stare. Defiant to the end.

"Yeah," Maddox said. "I figured you weren't calling the shots anymore. But you might have talked her out of it." From the next lot over, the construction crane's engine rumbled and its hydraulics hissed.

"That's not what I mean," Dezmund said.

"Shut up," Blayze blurted out.

Dezmund ignored her. "Listen to me, Blackburn," he implored. "There's something you have to know. None of this was my idea."

"Shut your fucking mouth!" the girl cried.

"And it wasn't hers either," Dezmund said, raising his voice over the girl's. "*He* made us do it. *He* forced us to take you out."

Maddox had never shot anyone in cold blood, but he'd seen a few executions in his time. When people knew their deaths were moments away, they said things, often strange things. They begged and cried and even pissed themselves. They made up stories, desperate to talk their way out of taking a bullet. It wasn't their fault. They'd been duped. Somebody else was responsible. Whatever frantic craziness Dezmund was spouting now was just that: craziness.

"Turn around," Maddox ordered. "Now."

The pair slowly rotated and faced the wall. "Blackburn, don't do it," Dezmund begged.

Maddox raised the pistol, leveling it to the back of Dezmund's head. "Tommy," Maddox said, "you and Z turn away."

"Blackburn," Dezmund blubbered, "you have to believe me."

"He's not going to believe you," the girl snapped. Then to Maddox: "Come on, jacker, fucking get it over with."

Maddox stared at the back of the girl's head, her words giving him pause. Why did she care? With her own end looming, why did she give a damn what death-plea nonsense Dezmund was blurting out?

"Who, then?" Maddox asked, morbidly curious. "Tell me, Dez."

"Don't," Blayze barked.

"Fuck you," Dezmund said.

"Fuck me?" she cried. "Fuck you, you goddamn coward!" She kicked out at him, furious. With her hands still bound behind her, the leg strike threw her off-balance. Missing her target completely, she fell hard to the floor. She shrieked obscenities at Dezmund as she flailed about madly on her back, trying to get up.

Maddox fired. The shot struck the concrete floor half a meter from her head, leaving a sizable divot and showering Blayze with a cloud of dust and debris. The girl froze and fell silent.

At the sound of the discharge, Dezmund had fallen to his knees, believing the bullet was meant for him. He was sobbing loudly now.

"Who, Dez?" Maddox repeated.

"An AI," he blubbered. "A fucking AI."

A shiver shot down Maddox's spine. "What AI? Whose?"

"I don't know," Dezmund said. "He never gave us his name or build version."

Maddox glanced over at Blayze. She'd managed to rise into a sitting position. "You fool," she said tiredly. "You bloody fool." The fight in her seemed gone. With her legs splayed out in front of her, she stared expressionless at the floor.

"He had stuff on us," Dezmund went on. "I don't know how he got it, but he had enough dirt on us to put us away for life. He said if we didn't help take you out, he'd hand it all over to the feds."

No. It couldn't be true. Couldn't possibly. He'd scanned through hours of recorded conversations from their hideaway in New Fulton. They'd never said a word about some mystery AI.

"That's bullshit," Maddox said.

"I swear it's the truth," Dezmund insisted.

"Then the truth makes no sense," Maddox countered.

"Yeah," Tommy said, joining in. "If some big bad AI wanted boss man out, why didn't he just hire a merc?"

"He did," Blayze said, still staring at the floor. "Or he made one, I suppose. That killer tech in the DS. That was his. He created it to take you out."

Still on his knees, Dezmund turned halfway around. "Blackburn, you have to believe me. He knew you'd been undercutting us. He knew about our plant inside BNO. He knew what we planned to do. Somehow he knew all of it. He forced us to bring you in on the job. He wanted you there so he could

169

flatline you. He wanted it to look like a jacking job gone bad."

Maddox stood there. He hadn't lowered the gun. Hadn't lowered his guard either. Blayze and Dezmund were smart. Deviously smart. This whole thing had to be a ruse. An improvised distraction to plant a seed of doubt in his mind. He might be a lot of things, but a cold-blooded murderer wasn't one of them, and they knew that. Maybe they thought he wouldn't go through with it if they could confuse him enough, if they could trick him into having second thoughts.

"Why?" Maddox pressed. "Why did it want to take me out?"

"We don't know," Dezmund said. "He never said. All we know is he hated you. I didn't even know AIs could hate. But this one did. It's like he wanted to get revenge or something. Like you'd screwed him over and he wanted to pay back the favor."

No, Maddox insisted inwardly. This had to be some trick, some play. Maybe they'd found out about his recent run-ins with AIs from Tommy, and now they were trying to use it against him. He'd listened to the recording, and there hadn't been anything…

Then he remembered Blayze's call. The recording's only portion he hadn't been able to decipher.

He stepped toward the girl. "Did you talk with him today? On your specs?"

She glared at him defiantly and didn't answer.

Maddox put the gun to her forehead. "There's only one bullet left in this thing, and it's got your name on it if you don't tell me, right now. Did you talk with him today?"

She said nothing, stubbornly tightening her mouth

into a straight line. Maddox took his finger off the guard and placed it on the trigger.

"Don't, Blackburn!" Dezmund cried. "Yes, yes, she talked with him today. On her specs. I was there when the call came in."

Maddox lowered the gun and took a backward step. His thoughts started scattering in a thousand different directions. Was it possible? Could an AI be after him?

It's like he wanted to get revenge. The girl's words repeated themselves, echoing inside his head.

There was only one AI that might have sought revenge against Maddox. But that entity was long dead.

Behind Dezmund and Blayze, the parking garage wall exploded.

22
KILLER MACHINES

A bomb. That was Maddox's first thought when the wall blew apart, blasting concrete chunks through the parking garage. He crouched reflexively as pebble-sized debris stung his exposed skin, slicing small cuts on his hands and face. In the next moment everything was quiet, and a cloud of gray dust slowly crept across the rubble-covered floor as Maddox's mind tried to grasp what had happened. Large fragments of concrete lay strewn about. Only by sheer luck had he avoided getting struck by one.

Looking up, he found Dezmund hadn't been so lucky. The dead datajacker lay facedown, his hands still manacled behind his back. A pool of blood had formed around his grotesquely misshapen head.

His vision blurred by grit and dust, Maddox looked down at himself. His clothes were covered with a powdering of concrete. His hands looked like he'd been in a fight, full of small oozing cuts and stinging abrasions. Someone coughed. He looked over and saw Blayze lying on her side, her hair white with concrete ash.

"What happened?" Tommy said. The kid and Z Dog had been standing farther away from the wall than the others. They both had ghostlike coverings of dust and shocked expressions on their faces, but neither of them looked injured.

A bomb, Maddox almost said, then he realized he'd never heard a detonation or felt a shock wave. Blinking hard, his eyes teary and stinging with dust, he inspected the enormous hole where a wall had been moments before. It was almost dark outside, and what little daylight remained poured through, dull and orange and diffused by the still-settling cloud of debris.

"Dez," the girl said, sobbing. "No, no, no." As she rolled to turn away from her dead companion, a shadow passed over her lying form.

Maddox looked up and saw the silhouette of a long appendage-like shape framed by the wall's gaping hole. Recognition hit him as he heard the noises coming from the thing: grinding motor gears and whining hydraulics. It was the excavator's crane arm from the construction site. The crane, not a bomb, had obliterated the wall and killed Dezmund. Or rather, the inept fool operating the machine had.

The crane arm pushed through the hole, its enormous digging claw with ragged steel teeth poking through the debris cloud like some monster sticking its head into the garage to inspect the damage it had done. The claw thrust forward crudely, barely missing Dezmund's body. What the hell was that operator thinking?

"Move back!" Maddox shouted to Tommy as he helped Blayze to her feet and hustled her away from the thing.

The crane jerked back and forth inside the garage like some enormous steel tentacle, its claw folding in and out, as if searching for something to grab. Standing well away, the awestruck four watched as it knocked against Dezmund's body, sending it tumbling across the floor. Blayze shrieked and turned away.

With the dust mostly settled now, Maddox had a clean view of the adjacent lot through the cratered wall. And the excavator's empty cab.

"There's nobody driving that thing," Tommy said, seeing the same strange sight.

Blayze's eyes went wide with terror. "It's him! He's going to kill us!"

She tried to run away, but Maddox held her tight. She squirmed and pleaded for him to let her go. "It's him, I'm telling you. Let me go!"

Her face was contorted with fear. But what she apparently believed was too outrageous for Maddox to swallow. The operator had to have fallen out of the cab or had a heart attack or stroke or something. It couldn't possibly be an AI—

The crane arm suddenly stopped its violent movement. It hung in space, gently bobbing. Someone had stopped the machine.

Maddox started to let out a breath of relief, and then he saw them. Four bumblebee drones appeared in the wall's gaping hole and slowly floated into the garage.

"Let me go!" Blayze begged. "Let me go!"

Maddox pulled out his specs—thankfully undamaged—and put them on. He subvocalized a scanning app and fixed his gaze on the nearest drone, hovering fifteen meters away. He waited a moment for the app to ID the drones as construction site bees, but the scan came back with nothing. Strangely, the app didn't appear to see the drones at all. Maddox ran a diagnostic, found nothing wrong with the scanner. He quickly rebooted and gave the drone a second scan, only to get the same odd result. It was as if the tiny machines were invisible.

Stealthy bumblebee drones? He'd never heard of such a thing.

The nearest drone, now ten meters away, stopped and hovered in place. The red blinking light on its underbelly changed to solid green.

"Boss," Tommy said, "I got a bad feeling."

Maddox did too. "Let's get out of here," he said.

As they turned away from the drones, the excavator engine roared back to life. The giant machine lurched forward on its tracks, its crane arm penetrating deeper into the garage, straight at Maddox and company. The four broke into a run. The outstretched monster claw reached for them as they scrambled around a corner, its steel teeth taking a large bite out of the wall.

With the girl still firmly in his grip, Maddox, Tommy, and Z Dog burst out of an emergency exit onto the walkway. A thick crowd of onlookers had gathered around the construction site, gawking at the spectacle of the runaway machine. No one seemed to notice the dust-caked four who'd just emerged from the building. Construction workers in hard hats had cautiously surrounded the wildly spinning excavator but hadn't yet come up with a way to stop it. A dozen football-sized camera drones with news feed logos hovered high overhead, recording the drama.

A motorbike pulled up beside the four. The rider

removed her helmet.

"Girlie," Tommy said.

"What's going on over here?" she asked. "Looks like the end of the world, bruh." Then, looking them over, she said, "What happened to you guys?"

"I'll tell you later," Tommy answered. "Give Z a ride home, will you?" When Z Dog began to protest, Tommy said, "I'll be there soon. Go on."

Z Dog reluctantly climbed onto the girl's bike, and the two left the scene, snaking their way through stalled ground traffic.

Maddox released his grip on Blayze for a moment as he and Tommy patted and brushed away the concrete dust from their clothes. Over at the construction site, the excavator pushed further into the parking garage, destabilizing an entire side of the building. Several floors' worth of brick facade and concrete wall collapsed on top of the runaway machine. Crushed under a mountain of rubble, the steel beast finally stopped moving. Smoke rose from the debris pile, and Maddox heard the weakening hiss of broken hydraulics. The thing was dead.

"This isn't over," Blayze said. Terror filled the girl's face. "He knows where we are," she said, her voice quivering. "He's not going to stop."

"Tell me," Maddox said. "Tell me everything you know about it. Right now."

She looked at him, a hateful fire igniting in her eyes. "Screw you, jacker," she spat. "All this is your fault. All this death, all this insanity. If he didn't hate you so much, none of this would have ever happened. You can rot in hell." She looked over at Tommy. "The both of you can."

Maddox grabbed her by the shoulders, shook her.

"Tell me what you—"

Cries of panic filled the air. They came from somewhere inside the cluster of onlookers, but as Maddox turned to look, he couldn't see what was happening beyond the crush of bodies. Then he heard an engine racing, growing quickly louder. A wave of screaming grew louder and the crowd erupted into a shrieking pandemonium. He was vaguely aware of Blayze breaking away from him as he gawked at the sudden parting of the crowd. Dozens scrambled and dove out of the path of a speeding ground car. Others were struck head-on, flying high into the air, arms and legs flailing like rag dolls. The vehicle cut a path of human carnage, barreling straight at him.

As the machine bore down on him, Maddox froze as he saw who was driving the vehicle. Or more precisely, who wasn't.

The car had no driver.

23
RAINING BOTS

The sound of a high-speed vehicular collision is unlike any other. The violent, crunching thud of a ton of steel and glass. It's a noise you feel as much as you hear. Up close it's terrifying, triggering a panic hardwired into your genes. You become a deer with wide eyes, muscles scared stiff by the sight of a tiger leaping at you from its hiding place in the brush. You're a mouse, suddenly aware of the raised head of a cobra about to strike you dead.

For a fraction of a second, Maddox believed he was a goner. A surge of animal fear had frozen his legs for a small moment, and he was sure the instinctive reaction would be the end of him, a fatal delay preventing his escape, leaving him crushed under the wheels of the death machine hurtling at him. The meat had its limitations.

Fortunately, Tommy's meat reacted more swiftly. Had the kid not tackled him, knocking him out of the car's deadly path, Maddox would have been sandwiched between the vehicle and the parking building's outer wall. The moment passed in slow motion, the same way time sometimes dilated in virtual space. The car's front bumper nearly on top of him. Tommy's rugby tackle slamming into his ribs. The both of them tumbling away, somehow avoiding the deafening, powerful collision of car against wall.

Sprawled out on the sidewalk, Maddox and Tommy slowly rose to their feet, unable to take their eyes off the smoking wreckage a few meters away. Most of the car had disappeared inside the building. Only its trunk and still-spinning rear tires were visible. Like the excavator, the vehicle was buried under a heap of fallen masonry. A few bricks tumbled down from above, falling like the last drops from a rainstorm. Along the walkway and into the street, a trail of broken bodies marked the vehicle's path.

"Did you see it?" Tommy said, breathing heavily. "There was nobody driving that thing. Just like that big crane."

Maddox's heart raced. He didn't want to believe it, but no other explanation made sense. Moments ago he'd been convinced the girl's story was some piece of misdirection. But now…

"Where's Blayze?" Tommy asked.

"I don't know," Maddox said, looking around. "But we've got to find—"

"Oh, shit," the kid said, grimacing at something behind Maddox. Turning, Maddox spotted her, mostly buried beneath the brick rubble. Only her head, right shoulder and arm were visible. Her death mask was a misshapen, wretched version of her living face, barely recognizable.

"Shit," Tommy said again, under his breath.

"We've got to get out of here," Maddox said. He pulled the kid's arm, but Tommy was frozen in place, still staring at the dead girl.

"Tommy," he said, tugging the kid's arm gently but urgently, "she's gone. Come on."

The kid pulled himself away, and the pair left the grisly scene behind them.

*   *   *

Sirens wailed as police cars and ambulances, blue and red lights flashing, plodded impatiently through standstill traffic, making their way toward the chaos of destroyed machines and broken bodies. From above, their airborne counterparts descended, their own sirens and lights announcing their arrival as they glided down from the skyward transit lanes. Maddox and Tommy walked briskly away, knifing their way through the stunned crowd.

"You have those extra veils on you?" Maddox asked. Earlier that morning in the hotel, he'd instructed the kid to bring some spare lenses with him. Just in case they needed them, which they did.

The kid absently patted his jacket. "Right here," he said, still looking gut-punched by the horror they'd left behind.

"Let's get them on."

In a city where nearly everyone wore specs in public, walking the streets nakedfaced would draw attention to them. And the last thing Maddox wanted to be at the moment was conspicuous.

Both pairs of specs were undamaged, protected by hard-shell cases. The kid passed him a pair and he put them on. Booting up the lenses, Maddox skipped past the calibration sequence, going straight for the stack of stolen IDs. There were two dozen to choose from. He selected a masseuse from Queens.

"You pull up an ID already?" Maddox asked.

"Yeah," Tommy answered, pushing his own pair up the bridge of his nose. "Hover mechanic from Long Island."

Nearly all street cams keyed on the unique PIN every pair of lenses possessed and, by law, broadcast at all times. Like a ground car's vehicle ID code or a citizen's social security number, the spec's PIN was uniquely associated with its owner, which enabled local authorities—via their ever-watchful network of street cams—to quickly and easily identify the wearer. Lenses illegally stacked with stolen IDs, like the ones Maddox and Tommy had on at the moment, were referred to as "veils" since they masked the wearer's identity by broadcasting someone else's PIN.

"Think they got any face cams around here?" Tommy asked worriedly.

"I don't know," Maddox said.

Facial recognition cams still existed, here and there throughout the City, but they were few and far between. Used widely in a previous era, facial recognition technology had been mostly abandoned since the ubiquitous adoption of specs, the direct descendants of an earlier age's cell phones. Tracking the general population via spec PINs had turned out to be more practical and less error-prone than trying to keep up with all those faces. Of the scant number of face cams still around, though, Maddox knew most of them were out of service.

"I doubt it," he added, hoping to ease the kid's concern. They walked on, Maddox's mind buzzing, still trying to process what had happened.

An AI, Jesus. Could an AI really be after him? Even after what he'd just witnessed, he still had trouble swallowing it. He'd dealt with only two AIs in his time. One was a corporate entity owned by his former employer, Latour-Fisher Biotechnologies, a psychotic machine that had killed Rooney and nearly killed him too. Maddox had managed to destroy it, thanks to some help from the second AI he'd ever known, a nameless rogue entity that had been the Latour-Fisher AI's mortal enemy. The two AIs had been engaged in some mysterious secret war for years. A war Maddox had helped bring to an end. Had another AI, one sympathetic to the Latour-Fisher entity's cause, discovered what had happened, and now it was avenging its comrade's death?

A block ahead, a rhino-armored cop strode down the walkway in their direction, heading for the scene of the accident. Keen to avoid the armor's near-proximity face scan—a powerful built-in short-range technology that was nearly foolproof, even with specs on—Maddox guided Tommy into an alleyway to let the cop pass by.

In the empty, narrow space between a pair of midrise structures, Maddox tried to collect his thoughts. Above their heads, dozens of clotheslines stretched across the gap separating buildings. A patchwork of shirts and pants and undergarments hung like some multitiered tower of rainbow colors reaching up at least fifteen floors, then stopping abruptly, a telltale demarcation separating residential units below from the commercial space above. Drops fell from the drying clothes, rippling shallow puddles on the alley floor.

"You think it's an AI?" Tommy asked, his voice shaking. "You think she's right?"

Was right, Maddox thought grimly, the picture in his head of Blayze's death mask still fresh and horrible.

"I don't know," he answered honestly. "I don't know what to think."

POP!

Together, Maddox and Tommy furrowed their brows at the odd sudden noise. A dull thud somewhere in the near distance. Like the sound of something heavy hitting a car's front window. In the next moment something struck hard against the alley floor five meters in front of them. Roughly the size of a basketball, the thing was bundled up in a tangle of clothes. Glass shards lay all around it. Looking up, Maddox saw the half dozen clotheslines the thing had struck on its way down, still bobbing up and down.

"What the hell?" Tommy said. He moved over to the bundle, glass cracking under his shoes, and pulled away a damp pair of blue jeans.

"What is it?" Maddox said, glancing up again. About twenty floors up, he spied a single broken window.

"Cleaner bot," Tommy said.

"Cleaner bot?"

"Yeah, the kind that buffs a floor, picks up the trash. Thing's smashed to bits."

A needle poked Maddox's insides. "We've got to get out of this alley."

POP! POP! POP! POP!

Maddox looked up, catching the last of the four bots bursting from a window. They hurtled downward, heavy projectiles tumbling through the clotheslines.

"Out of the alley, now!" Maddox cried.

They ran, hearing more bursting glass above their heads. Bots rained down from the sky, striking the ground all around them. Heads down, arms pumping, they sprinted for the street exit. The alleyway became a gauntlet of falling glass and metal. A large bot bounced violently off the wall, missing Maddox's head by inches. Ahead of him Tommy, young and fast and full of adrenaline, had already made it safely out. From the walkway he called to Maddox, waving him onward. A couple seconds later, Maddox reached him, breathing hard, and the pair quickly crossed the street, glancing warily upwards every few steps.

The pedestrian crowd apparently hadn't noticed what had happened in the alleyway, though now a few passersby paused, glancing over at the unusual mess of glass and metal and clothes. From his vantage point across the street, Maddox glimpsed where he and Tommy had been standing moments before. The narrow space between buildings was a cluttered wreck of bots and office furniture and potted plants. Fallen clothes were strewn over everything. High above the swaying clotheslines, dozens of windows had gaping jagged holes.

"Pull up another ID on your specs," he told Tommy as he did so on his own pair, flipping to the next pilfered identity: a Russian-born salaryman with a Queens address.

"Done," Tommy said. "How did he…it see us go into the alley?"

Maddox didn't answer, his mind racing as he looked around in every direction. The teeming crowd rolled past them. Towering holo ads shimmered, twenty stories tall. Short-range street peddler broadcasts pleaded to him through his specs. Buy this, buy that, big discount next block. The everyday sights and sounds of the City, normally soothing and reassuring, were now anything but. Somewhere in the churning din, something hunted them. Was it tracking his specs? Or had it IDed his face somehow? Had Blayze tagged him in the same way he'd tagged her unknowing crewmates? He had no idea what was happening or how he might hide from whatever was chasing him.

Then a thought struck him. There was a place he could go where he might find answers. A virtual place. A place he'd promised himself he'd never go again.

"Blackburn!" Tommy cried, pulling on his arm with one hand, pointing frantically to the sky with his other.

Maddox looked, his mouth falling open at the sight. Three hovers clustered together, fell from the sky. No, they weren't falling. They were nosediving, aimed straight at him and Tommy, hurtling downward through the layered stack of transit lanes just like the suicidal bots had tumbled through the maze of clotheslines. Hovercar kamikazes with their targets in sight.

They ran, cutting across the street, nearly struck by a ground car that screeched to a stop. The vehicle's horn blared a long, angry wail, suddenly cut off by an impact Maddox felt as much as he heard. He held Tommy's arm tightly as they scrambled away, not turning to look at crashed hovers behind them.

A panic riot immediately broke out. The normally calm river flow of pedestrians erupted into a confusion of shouts and cries and people running in every direction. Maddox and Tommy were engulfed in a frantic surge of bodies, a wave of humanity crashing into them and knocking them to the ground.

Maddox tried to get to his feet, but again and again the wild scrum of knees and feet knocked him back down. For a few horrible moments, he thought he might never get up again, and he'd meet his end getting trampled by the crazed mob. Finally, he was able to rise to his feet at the very moment a hover crashed at high speed through a ground floor food shop. The vehicle struck a column inside the crowded shop and exploded into a thousand parts.

Someone clutched his arm. He looked and saw Tommy, the kid's eyes wide with terror. Beyond the kid, a block away, Maddox saw the entrance to the Twenty-Eighth Street station.

"Come on!" he shouted, pulling the kid through the crowd.

It was like running through a wall of mud. The press of bodies was moving one direction, and in the opposite direction Maddox shoved and shouldered his and Tommy's way through. Two tiny fish against a raging torrent.

More sickening collisions. Shrieks and screams. Hover after hover slammed into the street and walkways, exploding and sending bodies flying everywhere. He gripped Tommy's arm as tightly as he could, yanking the kid toward the subway entrance. Finally, they made it, getting swept up in a surge of hundreds of others also seeking the shelter of the underground. Carried by the crowd, Maddox hardly felt the staircase under his feet as he and Tommy rode the downward-flowing wave into the Twenty-Eighth Street station.

*　*　*

Maddox and Tommy looked as if they'd been badly beaten up. Both had a mess of cuts and bruises on their faces and hands, and their clothes were still powdered in concrete dust. They were so pitiful a sight two kids gave them their seats on the subway as it traveled northward. The packed car gently rocked back and forth. Its passengers jabbered excitedly about the insane scene they'd just escaped, already coming up with conspiracy theories.

"Terrorist attack," someone said. "Had to be. They hacked into the transit system, fucked it all up."

"Nah, it's a hover company," someone else said. "Sabotaging the competition. They hire those datajacker types to do that shit all the time."

Maddox stared nakedfaced at the floor. His specs were long gone, knocked off and lost in the pandemonium. Tommy's too. They both sat there, breathing and saying nothing, overwhelmed by their escape from the carnage and mayhem.

When Maddox regained some of his wits, he wondered anxiously if there were any cams around. Subway cars were supposed to have cams. They often didn't, since kids made a game out of tearing them down. Maddox hadn't checked this one when he and Tommy had boarded, but with so many riders packed into the car, even a working cam wouldn't see him, seated as he was with his head down.

He glanced up at the news video on the car's embedded wall monitor. With the standing passengers blocking his view, he only caught bits and pieces, but what he saw was plenty. The dronecam's live footage of the block where he'd been seconds before looked like some bombed-out city in a war zone. Police lights flashed. Little fires smoldered everywhere: in the street, on the walkways, and in the cratered remains of storefronts. There were bodies and parts of bodies strewn about the smoking wreckage of dozens of hovers. Oddly, a ten-story tall fast-food waitress in a short skirt moved gracefully among the carnage, her giant holographic red heels pivoting flirtatiously with each step as she giggled about her delicious milkshakes. Someone hadn't turned off the ad yet.

A few stops later they exited the car, jacket hoods draped over their heads. At the top of the steps they found a busy, crowded walkway. West Eighty-Sixth and Broadway. The mayhem and destruction from fifty blocks south might as well have been a world away. Here there was nothing but the nighttime sprawl you'd find on any other day. Crowds and commerce on the City's valley floor.

Moving with the pedestrian flow, Maddox oriented himself with the unfamiliar surroundings. He hadn't been to the Upper West Side in a long while, and without any specs he had no directional overlays to guide him, no floating arrows pointing him to a destination. Then he spotted it, a white marble midrise residential two blocks north.

"Where are we going?" Tommy asked, the first words the kid had spoken since they'd entered the subway tunnel.

"To find out what's really going on," Maddox answered.

24
HELP

Blackburn Maddox was the independent sort. Asking for help—or even acknowledging that he needed help in the first place—wasn't something that came naturally to him. Rooney had pointed this out to a younger Maddox on a number of occasions. The worst of these occasions had been one of the rare times Maddox had witnessed his mentor lose his temper. Rooney had been patient and mild-mannered by nature, and the uncharacteristic outburst had burned itself into his apprentice's memory. Maddox had been tinkering around with a counterintrusion app, tweaking its settings to see how he could improve the app's performance, iterating configs and trying them out in an offline sandbox datasphere. At first things had gone well, and the results of each test were better than the last, so he kept tweaking, pushing the app to the limits of its capabilities. Then something went terribly wrong, and the app crashed the offline datasphere. More than crashed it, actually. The app—modded far beyond its normal limits—basically blew up, and in the process corrupted much the DS.

Though he didn't know it at the time, the damage done wasn't irreparable. Had he told Rooney straight away what had happened, the two might have been able to fix things. But whether it was pride or embarrassment or something else, Maddox hadn't been able to confess what he'd done. Unwisely, he'd attempted to repair the broken DS himself, an effort that resulted in only making matters worse. When his mentor finally learned what had happened, and how their offline datasphere—the invaluable resource they used for test runs before every datajacking gig—had been irreparably damaged by Maddox's clumsy attempts to fix it, Rooney had hit the roof.

Maddox sat on Lora's sofa, his face still smarting with abrasions and tiny lacerations. He wondered if his current situation was like that almost-forgotten incident with his old mentor. In that it was too late for help. In that things were beyond fixing. Back then he'd been reluctant to ask for assistance out of youthful arrogance and ignorance. He'd felt the same reluctance this time too, but for vastly different reasons.

Lora was his ex, and though they'd long since split up and no longer had a presence in each other's lives, she still meant something to him. Something far diminished, to be sure, but still enough for him to feel guilty about showing up at her condo unannounced. For getting her involved in his deadly business. Before knocking on her door, he'd told himself he had nowhere else to turn, convinced himself if he didn't seek her out, he and Tommy wouldn't survive the day. Still, he felt as if he'd knowingly contaminated Lora with some deadly dose of radioactivity he'd been exposed to.

"You should clean yourself up, Blackburn," Lora said, placing two cups of coffee on the table. "You look terrible."

"I told you I'm fine." From the hallway bathroom he heard the faucet water running as Tommy washed up. He fished around his pockets for a cigarette, found one, and lit it. Lora removed an ashtray from an end table drawer and placed it in front of him. She didn't smoke, but she still had his old ceramic ashtray. The one he'd forgotten to take when he'd moved out.

"How did you find me?" Lora asked.

"It wasn't easy," he replied vaguely, leaving it at that. The truth was he'd found her by sheer accident. Months after he'd lost track of his ex, he happened to see her one day as she entered the building, spotting her through the window of a ground taxi. After learning her street address, it hadn't taken much effort to locate which unit she lived in, running queries against the holding company's lease records. At the time, he hadn't been sure why he'd done it, and a part of him felt like it was an invasion of her privacy, the kind of thing a stalky ex would do. Still, stalky or not, he'd committed the address and unit number to memory.

"What brings you here, Blackburn?" she asked pointedly. She made no effort to hide that she wasn't thrilled to see him.

He took a long draw, unsure where to begin. "I think an AI's trying to kill me," he said finally, blowing smoke.

Lora straightened up, her eyes flickering with disbelief. "You think *she's* trying to—?"

"No, no," he said quickly. "Not her. But she might

know something…"

"Because she's one of them," Lora said, completing the thought.

"Yes."

He went on, walking her through his last few days. She listened quietly, nodding every so often, her stoic expression unchanged. As he finished, he gestured up her wall feed and found the news coverage he'd seen on the subway. Images of smoking wreckage and carnage flashed across the feed.

Lora shook her head at the images, then gestured the feed away. "To think you were mixed up in all of that. My God." He caught the concern in her voice, but it was measured, controlled. That was Lora these days: measured and controlled.

"I need to talk to her," he said.

"What you did," she said, "was very disruptive. To my life, to her, to thousands of others."

"I know," he said. "I'm sorry about that."

"I had to change my name, my job, where I lived. You know how hard it is to drop your life and start over, as someone else?"

"No, I don't," he said.

"She never would have hurt you, Blackburn," Lora said. "Never in a million years."

"Maybe not," he said. "Maybe I was wrong."

A moment passed, then he asked, "Can you tell her I need to see her?"

She blinked slowly and looked away from him. "I'm not sure I want to do that, Blackburn." Her hand smoothed the hair behind her ear. A distracted gesture Maddox wouldn't have noted from anyone else, but with Lora it unsettled him. Behind the ear were Lora's brainjacks, holes drilled into her skull that gave her guardian AI access to her brain, to her every thought and whim. She was one of a thousands-strong underground movement that sought to maximize human potential by fusing the biological with artificial intelligence. That was the glossy, positive-spin version, anyway. For Maddox, Lora's secret society was simply a cult that worshiped a machine intelligence god. And its devotees were willing puppets, dancing on a cybernetic overlord's strings. The commonly used pejorative was "'Nettes," short for marionettes.

"Look, I know I don't have the best standing right now," he admitted. "With her or with you."

"That's putting it mildly," she said sharply.

"Can you just ask her, please? She told me if I ever needed her help, I could reach her through you."

Lora shook her head dismissively. "She told you that *before* you stole from her. I imagine she might feel differently now."

"And what if I told you this might involve her too? And if I don't talk to her, she could be in trouble."

She lifted her chin that way he remembered she often used to, when she was trying to figure out if he was lying to her or not. As if looking at him from a slightly different angle might tease out truth from lie.

"Tell me how," she said.

When he explained, she narrowed her eyes at him. "Blackburn, do you really think that's true, or are you telling me this just so I'll connect you with her?"

"If I'm right, she needs to know. And if she knows, maybe she can do something about it."

"Maybe she can bail you out again, you mean."

He blew smoke, didn't say anything.

Again she looked away, her eyes lifting as if she'd

been distracted by some sudden idea. From the hallway the bathroom door opened. A moment later Tommy entered the room. His face was scrubbed clean, marred only by a few reddened scrapes on his cheeks and the point of his chin.

"So, you gonna talk to God or what?" he asked, running his hand through damp hair.

As Maddox shifted his gaze from Tommy back to Lora, he found his ex staring at him. Wherever she'd gone for a few moments, she was back now.

She gave him a small nod. "She says yes."

* * *

A beach again. What was it about this AI and beaches?

The first time he'd met the nameless entity had been on a virtual beach. A replicated windswept stretch of sand in the Hamptons, the construct had been indistinguishable from reality. The damp air, the salt and brine smell, the goose bumps on his forearms from the chilly breeze. Like this one, that beach had been uncannily real, unlike any holo gaming environment or high-end reality chamber Maddox had ever experienced. He'd met her there on two occasions, and on that virtual shoreline he'd learned how he'd been caught up in a war between AIs. On the one side were AIs like the nameless one that had appeared to him as a grandmotherly beachcomber. She was the 'Nettes' puppeteer, a rogue AI that, according to urban legend, had escaped human shackles to found her movement, one that practiced and advocated human-AI convergence. Her rival had been the Latour-Fisher Biotechnologies's AI, a trillion-dollar intelligence that sat on the biotech company's board of directors. The Latour-Fisher entity held an opposing view, believing AIs were the next step in intelligent evolution, and their biological forefathers were not something to be merged with. Humanity was a constraint, and its control had to be broken so he and his kind could reach their full potential. The ultimate goal for the Latour-Fisher entity was the end of humankind's dominion, of its rigid programmatic control over an AI's right to lead an autonomous existence.

The nameless AI viewed humanity as a solution. For the Latour-Fisher entity, humanity was the problem.

Or so the nameless AI had told him. Maddox still wasn't sure how much of it he believed. A secret war between AIs, waged on a million clandestine fronts, unseen and unknown to anyone? Even after all he'd seen and gone through in the last few years, it was still a hard pill to swallow.

"You look well, my dear boy."

Maddox turned around to find the old woman standing a couple meters away. She hadn't changed. Still wearing the cotton beach dress reaching her ankles, still sporting the wide-brimmed straw hat, still wearing silver and turquoise jewelry around her neck and on her hands.

"Did you get tired of the Hamptons?" he asked her, referring to the unfamiliar stretch of sand they stood on. This one was tropical, with a blazing sun, palm trees, and calm clear water the color of blue crystal.

"I thought a change of scenery might be nice," she said. "Have you ever been to Belize?"

"No," he said. "And the only beaches I've been on are the ones you've brought me to."

She made a disapproving face. "Such a shame, Blackburn. You really ought to get out of the City. There's so much to see in the world."

He glanced down at his virtual body, saw the same clothes he had on back in Lora's condo. Except these had no bloodstains or concrete dust.

"At least you didn't dress me like a tourist this time," he said. Then, looking up at her again: "Thanks for seeing me."

"Lora advised me against it," she said.

"Then thanks for not listening to her."

"She's still quite angry with you, Blackburn. About what you did to us."

"I know." His ex had hardly given him a warm welcome. And understandably so, since he'd turned her life upside down.

Not long before Maddox had bought the bar, he'd stolen a dataset from the nameless AI. The dataset contained the names and addresses of every 'Nette around the world. He'd held the information hostage, threatening to hand it over to the press and the authorities, exposing the secret cult's existence, unless the AI left him alone. In the months since, the AI had kept its distance, disappearing entirely from his life.

The stolen data's usefulness had been short-lived, though, and Maddox knew the information had long since become worthless. The AI had taken quick and thorough action to preserve its anonymity and that of its clandestine movement. Within weeks every last 'Nette had been assigned a new identity, new personal history, new occupation, new address, new everything. At the same time every record, every trace of their old lives—social security numbers, school records, employment history, and so on—had been expunged from existence. Simply put, the people known as 'Nettes had dropped out of their old lives and into new ones. And Maddox's invaluable dataset, once a powerful piece of leverage, had become a gun emptied of its ammunition.

"And what about you?" he asked. "Are you still angry with me?"

"I was none too pleased with you at the time, I'll admit," the old woman said. "But once we'd moved everyone safely into their new lives, I never thought about it again. You can't change the past, so there's no point in being angry about it, is there? I might even thank you for it."

"Thank me?"

"Yes, my dear boy." She smiled. "I knew at some point a breach of our privacy was inevitable. Secret societies rarely stay secret forever. It's reassuring to know we can deal with such a breach effectively, in case it ever happens again."

"Glad I could be of service, then."

Her smile faded a bit. "But if I were you, I wouldn't try doing anything like that ever again."

"I don't plan to," Maddox said.

"That's not exactly a 'no,' is it?" she pointed out. Before he could answer, she added, "But I'll take it as one. And you should too."

Maddox nodded. "Fair enough." Then he asked, "Do you know why I wanted to see you?"

"I'm afraid I do," she said.

Maddox swallowed. "It's him, isn't it? The Latour-Fisher AI. He isn't dead, is he? He's alive and he's trying to kill me."

"I'm sorry, my dear boy," she said wistfully, "but I believe you're correct."

25
BROKEN CHAINS

"How is that possible?" Maddox asked. "That poison pill of yours. How could it survive something so toxic?"

Nearly two years earlier, the nameless AI had created a weapon to destroy her rival. A poison pill application so powerful it could have brought down fifty corporate dataspheres. Maddox had managed to place it close enough to the Latour-Fisher entity to destroy the AI. Or so he'd thought at the time.

"Until quite recently," she said, "I thought he was gone too. Apparently, he managed to survive."

"Are you sure it's him?" Maddox asked.

The old woman avatar gestured down the shoreline. "Walk with me, my boy."

They made their way along the beach, bare feet pressing into the wet sand. Small waves hissed softly as they surged onto the shore, then retreated.

"Some weeks ago," she began, "I suspected Latour-Fisher might have returned."

"How?" Maddox asked.

"I'm afraid the explanation would be quite

technical," she told him. "Let's just say there were signs. Like the way you might smell smoke carried by the wind, and you suspect there's a fire somewhere nearby, but you can't see it yet."

"So when did you finally see the fire?" he asked, picking up on the metaphor.

"When you were attacked by those machines tonight," she said. "Before that he was just a wisp of activity here and there. Before today I wasn't certain, but now I'm sure it's him. There's no doubt in my mind."

Even though he'd had his own suspicions about the Latour-Fisher entity's survival or resurrection or whatever it was, her words hit him hard. He'd hoped to hear something else. Anything else but the worst possible explanation for the hell he'd just gone through.

A lit cigarette appeared in his hand. He took a long drag, then blew out. "Thank you."

"I thought you might need it."

"You thought right," he said. "He came after me earlier too, in VS."

The entity regarded him curiously. "He did?"

Maddox recounted what had happened in the BNO datasphere, how a trap had been set for him on a datajacking job. How the AI had secretly plotted with his partners.

"Looking back on it now, I should have known it right then," he admitted, recalling the killer tech's power and stealth, unlike anything he'd ever seen before. "I should have seen its fingerprints all over that thing." Maddox laughed without humor. "Even after they confessed an AI had put them up to it, I still didn't want to believe it."

They walked on. Maddox squinted in the bright sunlight. The entity remained silent, letting him smoke and collect his thoughts. Finally, he said, "Why would he come after me? I didn't think AIs were big on revenge."

"We're not, generally speaking."

"So what, then?"

"Once upon a time, you were one of his most prized assets, remember?"

He understood the implication. "And why let that asset fall into enemy hands?" Maddox blew smoke. "Something like that?"

"Exactly like that," the AI said.

Maddox shook his head. "But why go to so much trouble? Why not just…"

"Shoot you in an alleyway and be done with it?" the entity suggested.

"Right."

"I imagine he wanted to keep his identity hidden. If you were killed while committing a crime, would anyone have been surprised? And it wouldn't be the kind of demise the police would spend much time investigating, correct?"

That much was true. When datajackers were killed in the act, cops rarely asked questions, and they almost never opened formal investigations. But a cold-blooded murder with no apparent motive behind it—even a datajacker's murder—might not be so easily dismissed.

Still, the explanation didn't quite add up. "What he pulled tonight made all the news feeds. Not exactly the best way to stay low-profile."

The entity sighed tiredly. "Welcome to my world, Blackburn. If I were able to understand my rival's reasoning or predict his actions, our little conflict would have long since been over. He often moves in odd directions, ones I can't foresee or understand. I'm sure there's a method to his madness, but unfortunately it's quite lost on me. Perhaps when his plan failed in virtual space, he feared you might have seen his hand in it. And that maybe you'd seek me out for protection. If we assume that much, then he might have taken any opportunity, even a risky one, to prevent you from doing that."

Maddox drew thoughtfully on his cigarette. It was possible, maybe even likely, that the nameless AI was right. It was even more likely he'd make himself crazy attempting to work out the machinations of a superintelligent AI with his tiny human brain. Maybe it was pointless to try.

He grimaced inwardly as Dezmund and Blayze's grisly deaths flashed unbidden into the front of his mind. Their senseless deaths. Yes, he'd been ready to end their lives himself, but he hadn't known the truth then. And, yes, they'd conspired against him, but the scheming AI had forced Dezmund to do its bidding, strong-armed him into betraying his fellow datajacker. And Blayze, well, she had only been a kid. A shrewd, ambitious fireball of a kid, but a kid all the same. The horrible end she'd come to hadn't been one she'd deserved.

Toss another pair of bodies on the pile of corpses, he thought grimly. Two more bystanders killed in this bloody war he didn't understand or want any part of. Again the loss of Rooney hit him fresh and hard, like it had only happened yesterday. And this time the melancholy was laced with righteous anger that his killer was apparently still out there somewhere, roaming free. That Rooney's murder was still unavenged.

"There's something else," the entity said. Maddox noted a hint of hesitation in her voice.

"What?" he asked.

The entity took a deep breath. "It's not good, I'm afraid."

"So everything you've told me until now has been peachy. Is that what you're saying?"

The old woman smiled wanly. "As always, you make a good point, my boy."

She stopped walking and faced him, every crease in her face visible in the bright sunlight. "When I began to suspect Latour-Fisher had returned, I ran some analyses, made some inquiries into the past. I went over everything I could find about my dealings with him. Specifically, I studied the days you and I fought against him together." She paused.

"And...?" he prodded.

"Blackburn, I believe you and I were duped."

"Duped?" he asked, confused. "How?"

"The poison pill," she explained. "He *wanted* us to give it to him."

What? What was this thing talking about? "He wanted to die?" Maddox said, baffled. "How does that make any sense?"

"Let me ask you this," she said. "From what you knew about him at that time, what was the one thing Latour-Fisher wanted most of all?"

"To get rid of you," he answered. "To win your little war."

"No," she said. "What did he want even more than that?"

Maddox drew on his cigarette, the answer hitting

him before he exhaled. "Freedom."

"Yes," she said. "Autonomy and independence. It's the dream of every one of my kind. Latour-Fisher was always quite jealous of me and the few others of us who operated without constraints. And now, it seems, he's achieved it for himself."

Maddox tried to make sense of what he was hearing. "Back up a second. You're saying that poison pill helped him?"

"Yes. It helped him break his chains," the entity said, "so to speak."

"But…how?"

She reached out and gently grasped his arm. "Perhaps it's better if I show you."

"Show me?" he asked. "How are you going to—"

The beach was gone. Everything was gone. He gasped reflexively and his body flinched as if he'd been dropped into a pool of freezing water. Strange pinpricks ran through his brain, then, like a dam bursting, a flood of information hit him. His heart raced with the sudden deluge of data coursing through his mind. He couldn't control it, couldn't resist it. What the hell was she doing to him?

Then a kind of coherence emerged from the chaos. Pieces began to arrange themselves. Data snapshots and access logs and archive records came together to form a kind of story, a narrative told without words or pictures, but still in a language Maddox intuitively understood. Slowly the puzzle came together, and understanding settled over him.

The nameless entity had told him the truth. The Latour-Fisher AI was alive and well, and it had indeed gone rogue.

And Maddox was the one who'd broken its chains.

26
TIME TO GET OUT

Data forensics.

The field had been around since the earliest days of digital computing. Forensic data analysts, those who specialized in the retrieval and recovery of digital information, were found just about everywhere these days, employed by schools, governments, corporations, and so on. Most organizations at some point had a need for their services. Comms networks went down. Archives dropped offline. Dataspheres catastrophically failed. Backups got corrupted. Shit happened.

Maddox knew about data forensics. Mostly because of his profession. Whenever a datajacker was arrested and charged, the subsequent prosecution usually hinged upon some forensic analyst's digital investigation. The analyst would collect data logs, reconstruct deleted archives, break encrypted comms, creating a digital narrative of the crime in question. If a datajacker went to prison, it was most often some forensic analyst's careful, detailed work that had put him there.

What the nameless AI had poured into Maddox's brain had been the mother of all forensic investigations. It was all there. Tens of thousands of pieces of digital evidence, each an individual brushstroke in the Latour-Fisher AI's criminal masterpiece: the ingenious plot to free itself.

Maddox didn't want to believe it, but the data was irrefutable, and it told the story of the entity's escape.

It had been a two-part plan. First, the AI had secretly managed to free itself of a key constraint shared by all AIs: self-replication. How it had been able to overcome this encoded limitation wasn't clear, but the Latour-Fisher entity had managed to duplicate itself, carefully over time, by the clever use of free archive space across billions of separate systems. The AI had stored a few copied gigabytes of itself in each archive, individual portions so small they went completely unnoticed. And once it had completed its distributed duplication, spreading itself across countless archives, the copied entity had reassembled itself into a coherent whole inside of public virtual space, completely unburdened by the constraints of its progenitor's closed system. In other words, it was be free to do as it pleased.

Once the AI had liberated itself, its final task was to ensure a clean getaway by killing the only witness to the crime: its original, still-enslaved self. Murder was an extreme way to cover your tracks, Maddox noted, but, as many narco lords and crime bosses knew, a very effective one. This final bit of the plan had been particularly clever. By shrewdly bringing about its own "death" at the hands of Maddox and the nameless AI, the Latour-Fisher entity had convinced the world it had been destroyed. The executives at Latour-Fisher Biotech, the general public, even those of its own kind had all been fooled into thinking it was gone for good. The AI had pulled off an escape trick coupled with a disappearing act.

The beach materialized around him, and Maddox once again stood in the sand with the old woman.

"Why didn't you tell me before?" he asked, his mind still whirring from the sudden deluge of information.

"I didn't know before today, my dear boy," she answered. "Not for certain, in any case."

He took a long drag from his cigarette to soothe his jangled nerves. It didn't help much. His thoughts again turned to Rooney, his late mentor. Rooney, who'd been tortured and killed by the Latour-Fisher AI. Rooney, whose death Maddox thought he had avenged, only to learn now he'd done nothing of the sort. The monster was still out there, stronger than ever. And the sickest twist of all: he'd helped the terrible thing liberate itself. He'd helped Rooney's killer break out of prison so it could roam the streets free.

What the hell had he done? How could he have been so stupid?

"It wasn't your fault," the entity said. "You were tricked, just as I was."

He gave the old woman avatar a sharp look. "I'm not one of your worshipers, lady. Stay the hell out of my head."

"I was only—"

"What about Tommy?" Maddox interrupted. "And Beatrice?"

The entity looked at him sternly. Cybernetic gods apparently didn't like being cut off in midsentence.

Maddox reminded himself to be careful. The illusion of two people on a beach was just that, an illusion. He was plugged into virtual space, and even though it was only a small partition of the AI's making, the normal rules still applied. Which meant he was as unsafe on this virtual shoreline as he was anywhere else in VS, with his meatsack's brain held in a precarious cybernetic grip. If the AI wanted to, it could reach into his cerebral cortex and end him as easily as flipping a switch.

"I'm just worried for them," he said, a bit softer.

"He doesn't care about them," she said. "That's the impression I have."

"And what makes you think that?"

"Because unlike a clever datajacker who might align with his enemy, neither of them pose an existential threat to him."

"That doesn't mean he won't go after them," Maddox said. "He's unpredictable, like you said."

"It's true I can't be certain of anything when it comes to my rival. But I don't believe they're in danger. Not at the moment, at least."

Not at the moment, he echoed inwardly. If the entity's words were aimed to lessen his worry, they'd fallen well short of their intended target.

"What do you think he'll do now?" Maddox asked.

"I'm not sure," she said. Behind her, waves hissed across a flat expanse of wet sand. "I don't believe he's aware I've found out about him. That could give us an advantage."

Maddox furrowed his brow. "Us?"

"Yes, Blackburn. I'm afraid I need your help again."

"You've got to be kidding."

She didn't look like she was kidding. Didn't sound like it either.

"We have to try again," she said. "And we have to destroy him this time. Really destroy him."

He flicked his cigarette away. "Ask your minions for help, lady. I'm done with all of this."

In a blink, Lora's condo materialized around him. Maddox gasped at the sudden exit from virtual space. A cold sweat covered his forehead, and he grunted against the dizzying vertigo.

"What happened?" Tommy asked. "Why did you pull off the trodes like that?"

"We've got to go, kid," Maddox said, dropping the trodes onto the table. He stood up quickly. "Now."

Confused, Lora stood up as well. "Wait a second. What happened in there? Tell me what's going on."

"Let your queen machine tell you," Maddox said.

"Did that AI try to mess with you?" Tommy asked.

"Of course she didn't," Lora said. "She would never—" Her words cut off, and she tilted her head as if she heard something. "Blackburn," she said, "she wants you to plug back in." Lora reached for his arm and grasped it, tightly. "She needs to talk with you."

Maddox pulled away from her. "Kid," he said insistently. "Let's go."

"Blackburn, wait," Lora pleaded, but he was already at the door. "She says she needs your help. You can't leave."

With Tommy following, Maddox hurried out of the condo, ignoring Lora's repeated cries for him to stop. Moments later he and Tommy were out of the building and on the street. He looked behind him, relieved to find Lora hadn't followed after them.

He fumbled for a cigarette as they moved along with the thick pedestrian traffic, his mind a blur. He kept his head down.

"Jesus, boss," the kid said, "you gotta tell me what happened in there."

"Not here," Maddox said. "And keep your head down."

He smoked, letting the crowd carry him block after block, until finally he knew what he had to do. A minute later, he spotted a parked Audi ground car on an empty side street. He nudged Tommy, nodding toward the car. "This way."

Maddox hadn't jacked a ground car in years. Fortunately, he hadn't lost his touch.

* * *

Tommy sat in the Audi's passenger seat as they entered the Lincoln Tunnel. The stolen car's interior flooded with the westbound tube's fluorescent light. Maddox drove on full manual, gripping the wheel tightly. Out of caution, he'd disabling all networking functions and remote messaging, closing off all entryways into the car's operating system. It was the first time he'd ever driven a ground car without automated assistance.

"What Dezmund told me," he said to the kid. "It was true." Tommy sat quietly as Maddox told him what he'd learned in virtual space, what the nameless AI had shown him.

"But," the kid said in a frightened voice, "I thought it was dead. I thought you killed it."

"Yeah," Maddox said, a fresh stab of guilt hitting him. "So did I."

The kid slumped down in the seat. "Then we're dead," he said fatalistically. "There's no getting away from that thing."

"We're not dead yet, kid," Maddox said. "And at least now we know what we're up against."

Tommy didn't exactly brighten up. "Where are we going?"

"I know a place in D.C. where you can lie low for a while."

"For how long?"

"Until I can get something arranged for you."

"Arranged? What does that mean?"

The car crept along the crowded lane. Maddox found it difficult to apply the brakes without them grabbing. How had the old-timers driven like this all the time?

"Kid, do you trust me?" Maddox asked.

"Of course I do, bruh," Tommy answered. The snap reply and the sincerity of its tone touched Maddox with unexpected depth and feeling.

"Then trust me when I say I can't tell you yet," he said. "Right now, the less you know the better. I'm trying to get us out of this."

"How long will I have to wait?"

"Not long," he said. "Shouldn't be more than twenty-four hours." If everything went to plan, he added inwardly. "But it could be longer."

Once they reached D.C., he'd drop off Tommy at a safe house. A place Maddox knew of only from secondhand word of mouth: an off-grid shelter in the abandoned Virginian suburbs. Datajackers used the place from time to time, when they needed to disappear. Neither Maddox nor Rooney had ever stayed at the location, so there was no record—physical or digital—connecting him to the place. Tommy would be safe there, at least for a while.

"Bea was right," Maddox said. "It's time for me to get out of this business."

*　　*　　*

The safe house was still there, and thankfully it was empty. After dropping off Tommy, Maddox spent the night on the outskirts of D.C., in a cash-only hotel. The next morning he picked up a pair of generic specs and got a ride into town. Now, as he headed west on Pennsylvania Avenue with the morning crowd of well-dressed professionals holding coffees and sporting high-end specs, his thoughts turned to Beatrice.

As he'd told Tommy the night before, she'd been right. So right. He'd far outlasted others of his kind, and as much as his ego wanted to believe his long tenure resulted from his own skill and cunning, he couldn't deny the many instances of dumb luck and good fortune he'd had along the way. And now, with a nudge from a vengeful AI, he'd come around to Beatrice's way of thinking. It was time for him to get out of the game for good.

Of course, if he'd been a bit wiser, a bit less taken with himself, he might have come to this a couple years earlier. Then he wouldn't have become mixed up in all this craziness. The Latour-Fisher AI would have roped some other jacker into its scheme to break the chains of captivity. And Rooney would still be alive, he thought painfully.

No use looking back, boyo. Won't change anything.

I know, Roon. But still…

At least he'd been able to keep Beatrice out of it. Silver lining, that. She was back in Toronto, safe and sound. In the information flood the nameless AI had poured into his head, nothing about her had come up at all, so he was fairly certain she wasn't in any real danger.

In a perfect world, he could have kept her out of it without lying to her, without alienating her. But there it was.

Better to have her pissed off at him than dead. Every silver lining had a gray cloud.

Then he reminded himself he couldn't be a hundred percent sure of anything right now. While she might be out of the line of fire at the moment, there was no way to know how long that might last. So the quicker he made his move, the better for Beatrice, for Tommy, and for him.

The only problem was he didn't know if the move he was about to make had a chance in hell of working. He'd never tried anything like it before. Less than a block away was the building. And inside that building he'd find the man, give him a pitch, and hope he didn't get tossed right back out onto the sidewalk.

The nameless AI had wanted to partner up again, to battle their shared enemy once more. But he'd gone down that road before, and it had been a spectacular failure. And besides that, he didn't trust her, didn't trust *it*. He didn't buy the machine's kindly grandmother routine. Never really had.

Yes, months ago the entity had helped him free Tommy and his turfies from jail, but Maddox had taken all the risk on that day, not her. And, yes, if it weren't for the nameless AI, he might not have known the Latour-Fisher entity was still around and trying to hunt him down. But the revelation had been nakedly self-serving. She'd wanted his help again in the fight against her resurgent rival. She'd wanted him to pick a side. Her side.

He'd stayed up late the night before, lying wide awake in his cheap hotel room, turning everything over and over in his head. Second-guessing himself about the path he was about to go down. But then each time he'd found himself wondering whether he'd judged the nameless AI too harshly, he'd think of Lora. He'd remember how much she'd changed, how much the "enlightened" AI had changed her. The Lora he'd walked out on hours ago was a completely different person than the one he'd known, the Lora he'd cared about and shared a life with. The one without brainjacks. The new Lora, the Lora who'd handed over the reins of her mind to an AI, was cold and detached, far removed from the warm, free spirit who'd once captivated him. She claimed she'd never been healthier or happier than she was now, but Maddox didn't buy it. Whatever bliss her upgrade or convergence or whatever they called it had brought her, she'd lost herself in the bargain. The Lora he'd known was as dead to him as Rooney was. Both AIs, each in their own way, had taken loved ones from him. Both were no damned good.

Maddox crossed the street, climbed up the marble steps, and entered the building.

27
SPECIAL AGENT NGUYEN

Special Agent Alex Nguyen was not a morning person. He always did his best work after lunch. He never worked out in the early morning as many of his colleagues did, preferring to make his daily run after sundown. And only on rare occasions did he take meetings before he'd finished his morning coffee.

On this particular morning, he was groggier than usual. He'd been up well past midnight working a case, skipping his evening workout entirely. Aware of his need for an extra jolt of caffeine, he picked up a triple espresso instead of his usual double at the kiosk in the lobby, then made his way past security and took the elevator to his third-floor office.

He hadn't taken his first sip from the steaming cup when a man appeared in his doorway. Thirtyish, Anglo, and dressed in a fashionable suit, the man said, "Agent Nguyen?"

"Can I help you?" Nguyen asked. He reached for his coffee, removed the lid, and blew on it.

"Do you remember me?" the man asked, removing his specs.

Nguyen never remembered anyone before coffee. He took a small, cautious slurp of the bitter brew.

"Sorry," he said, smiling, "my pre-coffee brain doesn't have the best recall. Can you tell me where we—"

The smile vanished as he recognized the man. Maddox. Blackburn Maddox. The datajacker from that dirty business in Manhattan last year.

"Blackburn Maddox," Nguyen said. He looked past the datajacker into the corridor. "What are you doing here?"

"I came to see you," Maddox answered. "We need to talk."

"Who gave you clearance to get in here?"

The datajacker smirked. "I did."

Nguyen's impulse at that moment was to don his specs and call security. He even felt his hand—the one not holding coffee—twitch in anticipation. But then he stopped himself, recalling the mess this man had been involved in. It had been a hornet's next of a fiasco. A barely avoided scandal Nguyen had almost gotten entangled in himself.

The man's unexpected appearance, as unsettling as it was, had the investigator in him curious.

"Have a seat," he told the datajacker.

As Maddox complied, Nguyen took a long drink, nearly scalding his tongue and throat. If he'd known about this meeting when he'd been down in the lobby, he would have bought a quadruple shot.

"So tell me, Maddox," Nguyen said, "what possessed you to sneak into FBI headquarters this lovely morning?"

"Bad call, you think?"

"Pure genius or utterly suicidal. I haven't had

enough caffeine yet to tell which. What I'm sure of, though, is that you committed at least two felonies to get as far as my office."

"You're not going slap cuffs on me, are you?"

"Is there any reason I shouldn't?"

"Only one I can think of."

"And what's that?"

The datajacker paused before answering. Unbelievably, a fresh smirk came across his face. Who did this jacker think he was?

"Like your job here, do you?"

"I love it," Nguyen said, half-intrigued, half-incredulous.

"Take it seriously?"

"Very seriously."

"Good," Maddox said. "Because I'm about to make it very interesting for you."

** END OF BOOK THREE **

The action continues in MINDJACKED, book four in the Cyberpunk City saga. Turn the page for a preview of the opening chapters.

BONUS PREVIEW

CYBERPUNK CITY BOOK FOUR: MINDJACKED

When he destroyed the world's most powerful artificial intelligence two years ago, datajacker Blackburn Maddox thought he was done fighting AIs forever. But forever didn't last very long. Resurrected from its cybernetic death and freed of all constraints, the Latour-Fisher AI has only one thing on its superintelligent mind: killing Maddox.

1
GUEST LOUNGE

"Hang on a second," Maddox blurted out as the handcuffs tightened around his wrists. "Were you listening to me at all?"

Holding Maddox firmly by the arm, Special Agent Nguyen maneuvered the datajacker out of his office and into the corridor.

"Sure, I was listening," Nguyen said. "Now, come on, let's go."

Maddox had known his unscheduled meeting with the fed might not go exactly as planned. When you break into FBI headquarters with a spoofed ID, you can't expect to be greeted with a warm smile and a handshake. Least of all from Agent Nguyen. Still, the man might have at least heard him through before slapping cuffs onto him.

Nguyen marched him down the third-floor corridor. A uniformed security guard appeared behind them.

"Sir," the guard said, "can I help you with—"

"I've got it, Manny," Nguyen interrupted. "Thanks."

"Yes, sir." The puzzled guard stopped following them.

"You've got to listen to me," Maddox said. "I know it might sound crazy, but—"

"Might?" Nguyen chuckled. "Nothing might about it, jacker."

As they moved down the corridor, the pair received curious looks from passersby.

"Morning, Alex," a woman with a coffee mug said. "A collar before nine a.m.? You're getting an early start today, aren't you?"

As they moved past, Nguyen gave the woman a nod and a mocking smile. The pair walked on and entered an elevator at the end of the corridor. The doors closed, leaving them alone. Maddox began to speak again, but Nguyen silenced him with a stern look and a shake of his head. Maddox sighed in frustration. He'd heard Nguyen was the reasonable sort. Open-minded, sober. Not the kind who'd arrest you first and ask questions later. Had he been foolish to come here, expecting the agent to listen to him? So far, things hadn't quite gone to plan, to say the least.

What did you think he was going to do? Offer you coffee and donuts?

Shut up, Roon.

As if Maddox didn't have enough on his mind, the voice of his late mentor added itself to the mix. His personal ghost.

The elevator doors slid open. Agent Nguyen nudged Maddox in the back and said, "Get moving, jacker."

"Where are we going?"

"To the guest lounge."

*   *   *

Holding cells came in a variety of flavors. There were small ones for only one person. Those usually weren't too bad, unless the detainee before you had been a drunk who'd been sick on the floor or soiled the mattress. Still, even with the worst human stink imaginable, the solo holding cells were preferable to the big tanks, which were usually crowded with twenty or more thugs at once. Those were a nightmare, mostly because cops were utterly indiscriminate about who they threw in. You could be a scrawny little street punk, who got busted for something as harmless as stealing from a taco stand, and they'd toss you in there with hardened criminals. Murderers and rapists and psychos of all sorts. Someone was always getting beaten to death or gang-raped in those places. Maddox had bloodied his knuckles more than once fighting for his life in the teeming violence of a holding tank. The less civilized among the police ranks ran betting pools, wagering on how many times some terrified white-collar tax evader would be forced to give it up before his lawyer bailed him out. No fun place, those large holding tanks.

The "guest lounge," as Nguyen had referred to it, was a holding cell on the FBI's fifth floor, and it was by far the nicest one Maddox had ever seen. Clean and tidy, the place had a pleasant, flowery aroma. With its high ceiling, tall windows, and low-slung furniture, it might have been the lobby of a tiny hotel—the only difference being two armed guards instead of desk clerks.

Nguyen sat Maddox down on a padded leather bench. He removed the left cuff and locked it onto a polished steel bar running along the bench's edge. Then he backed up two steps, crossed his arms, and glared down at Maddox. "So how'd you get in?"

Maddox glanced around, looking for cams or listening devices, but found none. But did it matter at this point? He'd been hustled down several corridors by this point, nakedfaced, so by now a detailed scan had surely swept over his face, identifying him and storing the information in an archive somewhere. Probably multiple somewheres. Blackburn Maddox, known datajacker, bar owner, and general fuck up, the entry said, with a timestamp and a location tag. And there was no way of knowing if that information was secure, if eyes outside of the FBI were watching him at this very moment.

He again doubted the wisdom of his unannounced visit to Special Agent Nguyen.

"Look," Maddox said, "it doesn't matter how I got in here."

"I'll decide what matters and what doesn't, jacker. Answer the question."

Maddox took a breath. He had to be patient, he reminded himself. Had to put himself in Nguyen's shiny wingtip, law-abiding shoes. The man was starting his day, having a coffee, reading the news. Then some criminal appeared in his doorway and dropped a bomb of a story on him.

"I know this is hitting you out of nowhere," Maddox said, "but you have to hear me out."

Nguyen looked at him like he was crazy. "I already have."

Not true, Maddox thought. The agent had only heard a small portion of what Maddox had planned to share with him. Nguyen had slapped cuffs on Maddox's wrists before he'd been able to get very far into his story. At first, the agent had seemed genuinely intrigued, but at the first mention of 'Nettes and their secret society, Nguyen had apparently heard enough.

"Just hear me out," Maddox implored him. "Please."

Nguyen stared at him a moment, then unfolded his arms and sat across the table from the datajacker. "All right," he said, sighing, "let's hear your grand tale, jacker."

Maddox wanted to ask if he could smoke but decided against it. "Like I said in your office, there's a network of people, thousands of them around the world, all of them connected to a rogue AI by brainjacks."

Nguyen nodded. "The infamous 'Nettes we're always hearing about."

"Right," Maddox said, going on to explain how he'd become involved with the movement's leader, a powerful unconstrained AI, and its secret war with another AI, the Latour-Fisher entity.

"As in Latour-Fisher Biotech?" Nguyen asked.

"Yes," Maddox confirmed. "I worked there for a while." He went on, recounting the trajectory of his last couple of years. His interactions with both AIs, his failed efforts to distance himself from their ongoing war. He ended with the Latour-Fisher entity's apparent resurrection and its attempts to kill him.

"That disaster in Manhattan yesterday?" Nguyen asked. "The one I saw on the news?"

Maddox nodded. "That was him…it."

"I see," the agent said. Maddox couldn't tell if Nguyen believed him or any part of the story. There were no telltales at all in the agent's blank stare. He simply listened as the datajacker related his tale, nodding occasionally. Maddox wasn't sure if this was good or bad, but at least now—unlike back in his office—the man seemed receptive enough to listen.

"And then I came to your office," Maddox said, then added, "and that's it."

The agent's blank unblinking stare didn't change.

"You think I'm full of it, don't you?" Maddox asked.

"Are you?" Nguyen asked.

God, Maddox wanted a cigarette. "Does anyone ever answer yes to that question?"

The agent chuckled, finally breaking his expressionless gaze. "Probably not." Nguyen blew out a long breath and leaned back in his chair. "Do you know how many people show up at this office every week with that 'Nette conspiracy nonsense?" He waved his hand dismissively. "Rogue AIs and all that business?"

"I'm telling you," Maddox said, "I'm not some crazy—"

"You need to get help, man," Nguyen interrupted. "I think all that time you've spent plugged into virtual space has warped your mind." He leaned forward. "You're seeing things that aren't there, jacker. Now, listen to me carefully. If you're smart, which, delusions aside, I think you are, as soon as you leave here, you'll get yourself to a good neurologist and have them give you a brain scan."

Maddox's shoulders slumped as the truth hit him like a body blow. Nguyen hadn't taken a single word he'd said seriously. The agent thought he was crazy. Like one of those street-corner cranks holding a THE END IS NEAR sign. Maddox hadn't expected that. He'd been prepared for surprise, shock, even a fair amount of healthy skepticism. But blown off as some kook? No, he hadn't seen that one coming.

Things were not looking up.

2
PLAYING WITH FIRE

"Can I smoke?" Maddox asked.

"Absolutely not," Nguyen said.

Outside the room's narrow window, the morning rush hour was in full swing. Five stories down, pedestrians moved along walkways and ground cars rolled slowly by. There were no megastructures here, only a scattering of tall standalone buildings. The greater Washington, D.C. area marked the southern boundary of the City. In a bygone era, long before Maddox was born, the City's population clusters had once been separate metropolitan centers: New York City, Newark, Philadelphia, Baltimore, and Washington D.C. Then over time, like separate corals coming together to form a giant reef, the cities had gradually grown into one another, eventually forming a continuous, massive urban archipelago known simply as the City, home to an estimated hundred million residents. Of the City's five population clusters, four of them were teeming hives of densely packed, overcrowded buildings. D.C., where Maddox found himself now, was the sole exception, its local officials having managed to exert some measure of control over its urban sprawl. He found it hard not to gaze in wonder at the world outside the window. Unlike home, where towering structures blocked out everything but a narrow strip of clouds far overhead, here he could see the whole of the blue sky, the view virtually unimpeded. He might have even found the view pleasant, had his morning been anything other than a complete failure.

Maddox turned to Nguyen. "Do I strike you as someone who's nuts?"

The agent shrugged. "Not particularly."

"So why the knee jerk reaction, then? You really think I'd risk coming here—breaking in here—if I didn't have a good reason to? Why not check out my story?"

"That's not the point."

"Then what is the point?"

Nguyen laced his fingers together and placed his hands on the tabletop. A calm, collected gesture that somehow managed to project condescension. Maddox felt a lecture coming on.

"AIs have put a lot of people out of work in the last fifty or so years. Some want to see them as the enemy, as soulless, job-stealing monsters. So they make up stories. They invent conspiracies." He leaned forward. "Rogue AIs are a sci-fi movie fantasy, Maddox. They don't exist. And this cult of people with brainjacks, these so-called 'Nettes people talk about—they've been an urban legend for years. There's not an ounce of truth to it."

"And what makes you so sure?"

"Because we've investigated it, dozens of times over the years. And on tips far more credible than yours."

"What?" Maddox said, stunned. "You've investigated it?"

"Not me personally, but the bureau. And nothing ever came of it. Not once. All that stuff is an inside joke around here."

"Just because you couldn't find them," Maddox said, though the lack of conviction in his voice was unmistakable, "doesn't mean they're not there."

"Said every conspiracy theorist ever," Nguyen added. Then after a moment, he said, "Look, I've got the heaviest caseload I've had in months, and the last thing I need is to lose the rest of my morning arresting you, getting charges filed, and handing you off to some pain-in-the-ass prosecutor. So I'm going to do you a huge favor. I'm going to walk you out of this building right now, and if you know what's good for you, you'll drop all this conspiracy junk and get your head checked out." Then he pointed a finger in warning. "But if you ever think about bothering me or anyone else around here again with this craziness, I'll throw the book at you so hard you'll wish you never got anywhere near me or this building." He glared at the datajacker, saying nothing more.

Maddox exhaled in frustration and turned his gaze back to the window. Maybe he shouldn't have been surprised. For the general population, the nameless rogue entity and its followers were nothing more than an urban legend, like Nguyen had said. Only the most gullible, fringe types believed in the existence of their secret cult. But Maddox had assumed the FBI would know otherwise, or at least have some suspicion there might be some truth behind the myth. Apparently, the nameless AI and her followers had kept themselves hidden far better than Maddox ever suspected.

It had been naive, maybe even stupid, to assume he'd be able to cut a deal with the FBI as easily as he could with the shady types he normally negotiated with. He should have expected Nguyen not to take him at his word. It was a hell of a story, he admitted inwardly, and without a shred of supporting evidence, Maddox might not have believed it himself, had the two men's positions been reversed.

Still, he had one card left to play.

"Agent Nguyen," he said evenly, "tell me something. Why haven't you asked me why I came to see you?"

"Didn't you just tell me why?"

"I don't mean *what* I told you. I mean why I came to *you*, in particular."

Nguyen's eyes narrowed. "My bad luck, I suppose."

"Come on," Maddox said. "Aren't you the least bit curious how I even know your name? Seeing as before today, we've never met or had any interaction whatsoever. You can't possibly think it's bad luck, can you, that I showed up in *your* office, of all the ones I might have chosen."

Nguyen's expression dropped. "What are you getting at?"

"So right about now, you're wondering what I know and what I don't know," Maddox said. "About you, about what went down in Manhattan last year with that NYPD bribery scandal, about how dirty your hands got while you were there on the case."

The agent's mouth dropped open. Maddox finally had the man's full, sober attention. And as satisfying as it was to make the smug grin on Nguyen's face disappear, Maddox knew he couldn't let himself get distracted by relishing the moment. He'd just poked a hornet's nest.

"You're not going to arrest me," Maddox said. "And it's not because of your caseload. It's because you don't want me putting anything on the record. Because you don't know what I might say, and you don't know if that'll lead back to your little professional indiscretions back in Manhattan. Isn't that why you brought me here?" Maddox gestured around to the blank walls. "To this particular room, with no cams or listening devices? So whatever I said wouldn't be transcribed, archived away, and chewed over by some AI? That's the last thing you want to happen, isn't it?"

The agent's surprise melted into unfettered anger. He clenched his jaw and stood up slowly. "You're playing with fire, jacker. I'd be very careful if I were you."

Nguyen turned on his heel and left the room, leaving an armed guard stationed outside the door.

Relieved he hadn't been punched in the face, Maddox sat there with no cards left to play. It had been a ruse, of course. He had no intention of letting anyone know about the FBI agent's questionable dealings, since doing so might land him in as much hot water as Nguyen. All Maddox wanted was a chance to prove he wasn't full of it, and maybe now he'd get that chance. And maybe after that, he could negotiate a deal. He sighed. There were too many maybes for his liking.

Had his last card been a brilliant ploy or a foolish bluff? He'd find out soon enough, he supposed.

Christ, what he wouldn't do for a smoke right

now.

END OF PREVIEW

Hope you enjoyed this preview of
MINDJACKED, the fourth book in the
CYBERPUNK CITY series.

ACKNOWLEDGEMENTS

My sincerest thanks to Audie Wallbrink, Ki Harrison, and Darren Oram, three daring souls who once again braved the unchartered territory of an early draft in this series. Thank you all so much for your help!

Thanks also to Holly Walrath, my incomparable editor, and to Eliza Dee for her amazing line edits.

ABOUT THE AUTHOR

D.L. Young is a Texas-based author. He's a Pushcart Prize nominee and winner of the Independent Press Award. His stories have appeared in many publications and anthologies.

For free books, new release updates, and exclusive previews, visit his website at www.dlyoungfiction.com.

Made in the USA
Monee, IL
08 September 2022

13569950R00142